"If you come to work for me, I assure you, nothing will happen between us."

"Why would you think it would?" Joa demanded. Her back straightened, her mouth tightened and she tapped an index finger on the granite, completely irritated.

Good—irritation he could handle. This chemistry, however...

Ronan needed to push, to make sure there was no wiggle room on this. Nothing could, or would, happen between them.

"Look, I know you've been checking me out, that you're attracted to me."

He thought he heard a snort of amusement. But he couldn't miss the fire in her eyes. "I'm an almost-thirty-year-old healthy female who hasn't had sex in a while and you're a good-looking guy."

But?

"But the world is full of good-looking guys, Murphy, and I can take or leave them."

Now, why did that sound like a challenge?

* * *

Temptation at His Door by Joss Wood is part of the Murphy International series.

Dear Reader,

Murphy International, the world-famous auction house, is owned and operated by the Murphy brothers: Carrick, Ronan and Finn. In *One Little Indiscretion*, I introduced you to Carrick Murphy, the eldest of the Murphy clan.

Temptation at His Door is Ronan Murphy's story. Ronan's much-loved and adored wife died giving birth to Aron, the second of his two sons, three years ago. He was blindsided by grief and in his head and heart, he's still married.

Joa Jones, having left her au pair job in New Zealand, wants a new start. She's realized that, while au pairing gives her a taste of being part of a family, it's not enough.

Should Joa be nanny to Ronan's boys? They both think this is a terrible idea. Joa because she's terrified to fall in love with another family who will, eventually, move on without her and Ronan because Joa is the first woman he's been attracted to since his wife died.

It was so much fun pushing and prodding my two stubborn characters toward love and making them realize that who and what they need is right in front of them.

Happy reading!

Joss

Xxx

Connect with me on:

Facebook: JossWoodAuthor

Twitter: JossWoodbooks

Bookbub: joss-wood

JOSS WOOD

TEMPTATION AT HIS DOOR

HARLEQUIN
DESIRE

HARLEQUIN®
DESIRE™

ISBN-13: 978-1-335-20905-4

Temptation at His Door

Copyright © 2020 by Joss Wood

Recycling programs
for this product may
not exist in your area.

This edition published by arrangement with Harlequin Books S.A.

For questions and comments about the quality of this book,
please contact us at CustomerService@Harlequin.com.

Harlequin Enterprises ULC
22 Adelaide St. West, 40th Floor
Toronto, Ontario M5H 4E3, Canada
www.Harlequin.com

Printed in U.S.A.

Joss Wood loves books and traveling—especially to the wild places of southern Africa and, well, anywhere. She's a wife, a mom to two teenagers and slave to two cats. After a career in local economic development, she now writes full-time. Joss is a member of Romance Writers of America and Romance Writers of South Africa.

Books by Joss Wood

Harlequin Desire

Murphy International

One Little Indiscretion
Temptation at His Door

Love in Boston

Friendship on Fire
Hot Christmas Kisses
The Rival's Heir
Second Chance Temptation

Visit her Author Profile page at Harlequin.com, or josswoodbooks.com, for more titles.

You can also find Joss Wood on Facebook, along with other Harlequin Desire authors, at Facebook.com/harlequindesireauthors!

One

Joa Jones ducked under the red-and-white portico covering the impressive doors to Murphy International, thankful to get out of the snow-tinged rain. She blew into her hands, thinking she was inadequately dressed for Boston in late January.

It had been summer when she left Auckland two days ago. Left what she knew would be her last au pair contract.

In New Zealand she'd been an integral part of the Wilson family, welcomed and loved. They'd suggested she move to London with them but she knew that it was one of those oh-God-what-if-she-says-yes? suggestions. No, moving to London with the Wilsons wasn't an option; their kids were older now and no longer needed a nanny.

Sadly, Joa knew she needed to move on. She could've easily picked up another job in New Zealand but, for the last few months, she'd been unable to ignore the feeling that she was in the wrong country, and in the wrong career.

Returning to Boston was a scary but necessary option. The *only* option.

Joa pushed her fist into her sternum, trying to push her panic down.

Since Iz's death she'd done a load of self-analysis and was now self-aware enough to know that by becoming an au pair, she'd been trying to find the family she'd never had growing up in the foster care system. She was twenty-nine years old and if she wanted a family, she'd have to make her own.

And she was done insinuating herself into other people's lives only to have to say goodbye when the families moved on.

Returning to Boston was her new start, a reset.

She'd take the time to be with her foster sister, Keely, and with Keely's help, Joa could figure out what came next.

Blowing into her hands, Joa looked up and down the street, not seeing Keely. On arriving at Logan International, Joa had received a text message asking her to come directly to Murphy International, the world-renowned auction house situated in central Boston. She and Keely had a meeting with the CEO to discuss the auction of Joa's foster mother's (and Keely's great aunt's) art collection. The collection was one of the best in the world and, on Isabel

Mounton-Matthew's death a little over a year ago, Joa and Keely inherited her art, along with a historic house in Boston's moneyed Back Bay neighborhood, a stupendously healthy stock portfolio and various plump bank accounts.

Joa, a child of Boston's foster care system and a teenage runaway, was now an heiress. The mind boggled.

Keely, adopted by Isabel after her parents' deaths when she was little, could've just met with Carrick Murphy on her own; she knew the Murphy brothers from way back and Joa had given her power of attorney to act on her behalf a week after Iz died. She trusted Keely implicitly.

But Boston was where Joa needed to be, the place where she would—she hoped—figure out her future.

A taxi pulled up and then Joa found her arms full of her curvy, bubbly friend. Keely rained kisses on her face. "It's so amazing to see you, Ju. FaceTime is just not the same."

"It's good to see you too, Keels," Joa quietly told her. And it was.

This woman had welcomed Joa into her house, into her life, and treated her like a sister, a best friend. From the day she'd left the shelter and moved into Isabel's mansion, Keely had shared her clothes, showed her how to apply makeup, coached her through her first date. It was Keely who'd helped her fill in college applications and choose her prom dress.

Most importantly, it was Keely who held her hand as they buried Isabel.

Impulsively and uncharacteristically, Joa reached for Keely again and pulled her into another hug. She was family; the only one she had.

Keely, always happy to hug, rocked her from side to side before pulling back and placing her hands on Joa's cheeks. "You're an ice block! For goodness' sake, let's go in. And what are you wearing?"

Joa looked down at her thin coat, jeans and now-wet trainers. "Not enough, apparently." She followed Keely into an impressive hallway dominated by a wide marble staircase and the familiar smell of beeswax polish.

To the right of the staircase, a sleek woman sat behind an equally smooth desk, waiting for them to approach. Keely pulled off her cashmere coat and draped it over her arm. A security guard stood by the door, another two by the entrances of the viewing rooms. Paintings hung on the walls and massive, tumbling arrangements of flowers spilled from two crystal vases on two plinths on either side of that impressive marble-and-wrought-iron staircase.

Joa, in off-the-rack clothes and shoes and wearing a battered vintage jacket, was in no doubt she'd stepped into another world. In spite of her new inheritance, this was Isabel's world, Keely's world, not hers. Intellectually she knew that she was a now stupendously wealthy woman, but emotionally, she was still that fourteen-year-old runaway, scared and cynical, always looking for the stick behind the carrot. A large part of her was still waiting for someone, anyone, to tell her that Isabel's bequest was a mistake, that a girl from the wrong side of the tracks wasn't allowed to inherit a half share of one of the biggest fortunes in the country.

Joa felt Keely's hand on her back, grounding her.

"It's so good to have you back, darling. How long are you staying?"

"Not sure." Joa moved her rucksack to her other shoulder and shrugged. "My contract in Auckland ended. I think I need to switch directions, find a new career. So I'm staying until I can figure stuff out. Is that okay?"

Keely pretended to think. "Well, I'm not sure if we have room for you at the inn. It's only a turn-of-the-century, fifteen-bedroom house with too many reception rooms, libraries, a ballroom, two dining rooms, a media room and servants' quarters. I'm not quite sure where we'll find a place for you," Keely joked. Looking at her rucksack, she frowned. "Where is your luggage?"

Joa pulled a face. "The airline lost it. I think it's in Kuala Lumpur. I've been told it will be here the day after next."

"Or never."

"That's a distinct possibility," Joa agreed.

Keely's phone rang and she dug in her tote bag to pull it out. She swiped the screen and Joa caught the indistinct outline of a handsome face, a flash of white teeth as the man smiled.

"Hey, where are you?"

Joa started to step away but Keely's hand on her arm kept her in place. Who was this man with the amazing, growly, gorgeous voice? Keely's new boy-friend?

Curious, Joa angled her head and, making sure to keep out of the eye of the camera, took a quick peek at Keely's screen.

Holy crap, cupcake.

Joa looked past the frustration dancing in those mostly green eyes—a light green touched with flecks of blue, gold and jade, the colors of a mother-of-pearl shell—and the annoyance tightening his mouth. Stubble covered a strong jaw and stubborn chin, and his open-collar chambray shirt skimmed broad shoulders, revealing a chest lightly covered with nut-brown hair, the same color as his collar-length, wavy hair. He looked like a fallen angel, someone who could be pretty but wasn't, and was better looking for it.

He rocked the word *masculine* and Joa just knew that his body would match his face. God couldn't be that cruel to team such a sexy face with a body that wasn't as fine. Joa was very certain he had a flat stomach, long legs and a perfect ass.

That was the only scenario that made sense. The butterflies in her stomach flapped their wings in enthusiasm. And appreciation.

When last had she had such a visceral, *sexual* reaction to a man? Last year? Two years ago?

Never might be closer to the truth.

"I've just arrived at Murphy's," Keely replied. "We're running late but I let Carrick know." Keely handed an appointment card to the concierge and motioned Joa to lead them up the steps. "Are you joining us for the meeting?" she asked the hottie on the screen.

"Nah, too much on my plate."

Keely stopped halfway up the stairs and Joa, a step higher, turned around to look down at her. A frown pulled Keely's delicate brows together and concern flashed in her eyes. The man on the other side of the call was someone Keely cared about.

"What's the matter?" Keely demanded.

"Anna's gone."

Joa, knowing they wouldn't be moving until Keely finished her conversation, placed her arms on the railing and looked down into one of the viewing rooms. Murphy staff, dressed in red golf shirts and chinos, carefully lifted a huge painting off the wall.

Keely sounded horrified. "Oh, crap, that's the sixth one you've lost since Lizbeth retired."

Sixth what?

"Tell me something I don't know." The voice muttered, utterly pissed. "She went on a shopping spree."

Keely pulled a face. "What did she buy?"

"Lingerie, designer. Cosmetics, designer. A designer sofa. Various high-end perfumes, shoes, handbags, clothes."

"Wait! Let me guess...all designer."

"Yeah. I single-handedly kept more than a few Boston boutiques in business recently."

"I would not have expected her to do that." Keely placed her hand on her hip. "You have the worst luck in nannies, Ro."

Joa's interest was pricked by the word *nanny*. It

was her profession after all. Ah, the conversation was starting to make a little more sense.

And Keely called him Ro…

Keely had to be talking to Ronan Murphy.

Keely had often mentioned him in her frequent, lengthy emails. He was the worldwide director of sales and marketing and Murphy International's chief auctioneer. Keely had known the Murphy family since they were all kids, and she had been a college friend of his wife's.

"I don't need this now. Thandi's parents are on vacation, so they can't help me with the boys and I have a day from hell today."

"I can pick them up from school, spend the afternoon with them and feed them dinner," Keely offered, as generous as ever. "They seemed to enjoy themselves last week."

"Isn't your sister coming in today?" Ronan asked.

"She's here." Keely started to turn the camera toward her and Joa made a slashing motion across her face. Was Keely insane? Joa looked like roadkill.

Keely rolled her eyes but thankfully didn't turn the camera. "Joa won't mind, she loves kids."

She did love kids, but on her first night back in Boston, she wanted to chat with Keely, drink wine, catch up.

Keely ignored Joa's shaking head, her don't-do-it expression. "Consider it done."

Dammit, Keels.

"You are an absolute lifesaver." Joa heard the gratitude in his voice.

"I'll let the school know," Ronan told Keely. "Now I need to start hitting the phones to track down a new nanny."

Boston had some good agencies; he'd pick up someone in a heartbeat. Joa knew this because she'd researched those agencies back in New Zealand, before she'd decided the Wilsons would be her last au pair job.

Keely tipped her head to one side, her bright blue eyes meeting Joa's. "Before you hire someone new, talk to me first. I have an idea."

The temperature of Joa's blood dropped a degree. No way, Joa mouthed. Absolutely not!

"If you are offering to look after the boys on a full-time basis, my answer is yes. Hell, yes."

Keely laughed at Ronan's hopeful statement. "I love you, and your kids, but not that much and not in that way."

So Keely and Ronan weren't romantically or, eek, sexually involved. And why did that make Joa happy? She was, obviously, more tired than she thought.

Keely continued, "But I might have a solution for you. Let me talk to someone and I'll get back to you."

No, she was exhausted and imagining things. Keely couldn't possibly have hired her out on her first day back home. Not even Keely was that bold.

Joa was done with au pairing; she didn't want to drop herself into another family because she couldn't trust herself not to fall back into her bad habit of pretending it was all real.

After Keely said goodbye to Ronan, Joa gave

Keely the stink eye. She wasn't interested in becoming Ronan Murphy's nanny, or anybody's nanny. Not today, tomorrow or anytime in the future.

"Do not even think about it!"

"What?" Keely asked, pulling on her butter-wouldn't-melt-in-my-mouth expression. Joa knew her better than anyone and knew a diabolical mind lived under that innocent exterior.

"I don't want to be a nanny again, Keels."

She was done with au pairing, with pretending she was part of a family only to realize that after a year, sometimes two, her families would move on… without her.

Besides, she didn't work for single dads, not anymore. She'd learned her lesson with Liam, then with Johan. Joa knew that single dads were her kryptonite, because she found herself easily believing she was the wife they needed, the mother their children craved.

Liam had met and married someone from his office, someone who adored his kids and was happy to be their full-time mom. The week before their wedding, Joa had gotten her marching orders. And Johan, well, he was gay and had wanted another husband…

If Joa wanted a family, she needed to have one of her own and not appropriate someone else's.

They started to walk up the stairs, Keely's high heels clicking on the expensive marble. Joa could only hope that she wasn't trying to figure out a way to get her to fall in line with her wishes… Keely was a force of nature. Not a gentle breeze or soft summer rain but a Category 5 hurricane or an asteroid strike.

Maybe if she changed the subject Keely would be distracted. It was worth a try.

"I know that Murphy's is going to auction Iz's art collection for us, but I don't understand the reason for this meeting. They have the inventory, they auction it off and then cut the foundation a check. I thought it was a simple process."

"Not exactly," Keely said, guiding Joa down the hallway to her right. "Murphy's has to check provenances to make sure all the items are genuine. Most of Isabel's works have been well documented, but Finn, the younger Murphy brother, found three paintings at Mounton House that we suspect might be lost Homers."

Okay, wow. This was news. "As in Winslow Homer?"

"Mmm. Finn Murphy took one look at them and said we need to establish provenance, which is a pain in the butt. Anyway, the meeting is with Carrick Murphy and Sadie Slade, an art detective. Isn't that a fun career? *Hi, I'm an art detective…*"

Keely continued to talk. "I did some research on Sadie and she's super smart and, unfairly, as beautiful as she is brainy. She's very much Carrick's type."

Joa rolled her eyes at the speculation in Keely's eyes. Her sister was both lovely and an impossible know-it-all.

Annoyingly, she was often right.

But Keely also had a grasshopper mind and tended to veer off subject. "We were talking about the paintings, Keels."

"Right, we need Sadie to tell us that all three paintings are by Homer. First, because they could raise a lot of money for the foundation but also because I do not want to eat crow."

Joa knew she was exhausted but she kept losing track of this conversation. "Why?"

Keely pouted. "Because snotty Seymour gave me a twenty-minute lecture about managing my expectations. He's the biggest pain in the ass. He's a lawyer's lawyer, a real dot-your-t's-and-cross-your-i's type."

Seymour? Seymour... Right, the lawyer handling Isabel's estate. Joa had met him at the funeral, then at the reading of the will. Grief-stricken, she hadn't paid much attention, and didn't remember much from either occasion.

"Isn't that a good thing in a lawyer?" Joa asked, bemused.

"I suppose," Keely admitted, "but he just annoys the hell out of me."

Joa was curious to find out how he'd managed to elicit such an extreme reaction from her I-bother-men, they-don't-bother-me sister. "What's he ever done to you?"

"He has a stuffy name and it suits him. Seven feet tall, six feet wide, blue eyes, dark blond hair, a long scar on his jawline. His friends call him Dare, an equally stupid name."

Okay, as their lawyer, his looks and a nickname shouldn't be a factor. Keely had obviously spent a lot of time looking at the face of someone who annoyed her. Interesting.

Keely stopped by a door with a discreet plate stating it was the conference room—thank God!—and Joa prayed that someone behind the expensive door would offer her coffee. And lots of it.

Joa pushed her shoulders back. She was here so she'd attend this meeting but then she'd retreat, leaving Keely to operate in this rarified world of high-priced estate lawyers and world-renowned auctioneers. Her job, her priority, was to redesign her life...

And if that was her plan, and it was a good one, then why did Ronan Murphy's masculine face keep popping onto the big screen of her mind?

Two

Down the passage from the conference room, Ronan Murphy heard the beep of an incoming group message and picked up his cell phone. Seeing the name of the parents' group for his sons' school in West Roxbury, he opened the message and saw it was a reminder about a dance the fund-raising committee was hosting at the end of the month. God knew why they needed to raise funds—the school fees he paid should cover everything from buying plutonium for science experiments to European white truffles for staff lunches.

His phone lit up as message after message came in and Ronan recognized some of the profiles as he'd met many of the mothers while doing the school run. He'd also made the mistake of engaging a few of them in conversation. A few casual greetings and some exchanges about the weather morphed into suggestions of playdates for their kids and a heartbeat or two later, blatant offers to buy him coffee, wine or dinner. He'd even had a few offers for some bed-based fun.

They all received his "I appreciate the thought but I'm not currently dating" line and a few told him to call them if he changed his mind. He wouldn't.

His wife was gone but she was still his wife…

Ronan ran his hand over his jaw, ignoring his cramping heart. He couldn't think of Thandi now, he had work to do, a list as long as his arm to get through. And top of his list was finding a new nanny for his boys.

If he cared what anyone thought, he'd be embarrassed by his inability to hold on to a nanny but since he didn't, he wasn't. As Keely recently reminded him, he'd been through six nannies since Lizbeth retired eighteen months ago, with none of them sticking. Mostly because they paid him more attention than they did his kids.

He didn't need their attention and affection, his boys did.

All he wanted was a nanny who didn't hear the Murphy name and immediately think *"ding, ding, ka-ching, rich Boston bachelor."* Four of the six nannies had flirted like crazy, with two being honest and upfront, telling him that sex was also included in the list of services they provided. Three years had passed since Thandi's death, but he still felt married. He didn't cheat: never had, never would.

He'd thought he was safe from further machinations when he hired Anna—she told him she was gay and in a relationship—but her unauthorized usage of his credit card was theft and couldn't be overlooked.

He wanted someone who didn't steal from him, who didn't see him as a potential husband or lover. He just wanted someone dedicated and honest, someone who'd walk into his house and do what he'd asked them to: look after his kids and leave him alone.

Really, was that so much to ask?

Eli, his executive assistant for the last two years, rapped on his door, and stepped into the room when Ronan told him to enter. Ronan closed one eye at Eli's flame orange suit and black tie. Eli was not only a kick-ass assistant, he was also very fashion forward.

Very, very fashion forward.

Ronan closed his eyes and made a show of patting his desk. "Help, where are my sunglasses?"

Eli rolled his eyes, made to look bigger with a hint of eyeliner. "I'll have you know that fire orange is in fashion."

"Where? In prison?" Ronan shot back.

Eli skimmed the folder across his desk and Ronan stopped it tumbling off the edge by slapping his hand on top. Ronan checked Eli's expression and was relieved to see amusement dancing in those faded blue eyes. He frequently gave Eli crap about his clothes but he never wanted to hurt his feelings. Thankfully, Eli seemed to take his comments with a grain of salt.

Ronan leaned back in his chair and placed his feet on the corner of his desk. He linked his hands across his stomach and rested the back of his head on the seat. "I need to find another nanny. Can you call the agencies for me?"

Eli didn't react. "Sure. What happened this time?"

Ronan explained and Eli shook his head. "I'll get on it." He nodded at the folder under Ronan's hand. "That's an updated list from Finn, detailing the contents of Isabel Mounton's collection. It's quite impressive."

Ronan had already read the updated inventory but didn't tell him that. Eli dropped into the chair on the opposite side of his desk and they ran through Ronan's massive to-do list. With Ronan overseeing Murphy International's worldwide publicity campaigns and their many client liaison divisions, there was never a shortage of work.

"Headache?" Eli asked, seeing Ronan rub his temples with his fingertips.

Always. "Yeah. Got any painkillers?"

Eli shook his head. "You used the last of my stash yesterday. I was going to pick up more later."

Dammit. He thought there might be some pain tablets in the executive bathroom off the company gym. But only he, Carrick and Finn had access.

Ronan pushed his chair back and stood up. The sooner he killed his headache, the sooner he could make a dent in his to-do list. He told Eli to contact the nanny placement agencies while he was gone and left his office.

He passed the conference room, deep in thought. How could he balance his work obligations with his kids? Sure, he could work from home in the interim but that wasn't a long-term solution. He needed, dammit, help.

He needed another Lizbeth…

Ronan heard someone calling his name, silently cursed and turned around. He jammed his hands into his olive green chinos, pulling a smile up onto his face. When he realized it was Keely who'd called him, his smile turned genuine.

Keely was one of his favorite people. Frankly, he didn't know what he would've done these past years without her. She was part best friend, part sister, all good.

Keely reached him and Ronan dropped a kiss on her cheek. "Hey, you. Thanks again for helping me out today." Her meeting with Carrick and the art detective must've just ended. "How goes the authentication process?"

Keely pouted. "Slowly. And it looks like only one of the three paintings might be a Homer, the other two aren't good enough."

"That's not a surprise since Finn raised the same concerns when he first saw the paintings at Mounton House."

Keely nodded and, without turning around, reached back, grabbed the sleeve of a leather jacket and tugged her companion forward. "I've been dying for you two to meet. It's ridiculous that you haven't been introduced long before this. Ro, this is Joa."

He'd heard about her, sure, but they'd never crossed paths. When they were younger, it was because Joa was less socially active than Keely and did her own thing. After school, she went out of state for college and as soon as she graduated, she started to travel.

Keely had described Joa—pronounced Ju-ah, he had to remember that—as having some Bengali ancestry, and he'd imagined a woman with straight dark hair and equally dark eyes. Keely mentioned that she was pretty but he'd never expected her beauty to whip his breath away. Keely also failed to inform him that her eyes were the color of moonlight, a pure clear silver, a color beyond description. Ronan had no doubt those eyes would change depending on her mood: would they turn to pewter, to ash gray, to smoke?

Ronan broke their stare and resisted the urge to run his hand across his face. She didn't need to see how much she'd rocked his world, how off-kilter he felt.

But the truth was… God, she was exceptional.

The rational part of his brain made a quick list— high cheekbones, a mouth made for French kissing and black hair, long and straight and thick, tucked behind pretty little ears—but most of his brainpower was engaged in keeping himself from yanking her into his arms.

Desire, hot and foreign, flickered to life. Heat curled down his spine. Ronan swore that if he licked his finger and placed it against his skin, he would sizzle. He'd never, not even with Thandi, had such a visceral reaction to a woman before.

It made him feel a little sick and a lot sad.

Ronan, knowing that he couldn't keep acting like an idiot, told himself to pull it together. He knew how to talk to people, dammit; it was what he did for a living. He slid another smile onto his face and held out his hand.

Joa tipped her head to one side and put her hand in his. Ribbons of pleasure-pain shot through his fingers up his arm. Pleasure because her hand was soft and feminine, pain because he knew this was the only time he'd ever touch her.

He was married; Thandi was the love of his life. Love and loyalty didn't die just because death separated them. Ronan and Joa exchanged polite inanities for a minute and Ronan noticed she seemed to be finding it difficult to break their eye contact.

Good to know this madness wasn't one-sided.

Keely, bumping his arm with her shoulder, interrupted their eye-lock. "I'm so glad I caught you, Ronan. Where were you rushing off to?"

Ronan gave her a blank look. "I was rushing?"

"You stormed past Joa, you didn't even notice her standing there," Keely said.

He hadn't? How was that even possible? And damn, why couldn't he remember where he was going? Oh, that might be because his brain had just been fried by a thousand volts.

"Did you call the agencies to send you a new batch of nannies to interview?" Keely asked him.

Concentrate, Murphy. "No, Eli is working on that now."

Keely grinned at him. "Tell him not to bother, I have another plan. A really good plan."

"What plan?" Ronan asked, his tone wary. He didn't trust Keely's super innocent expression.

"Ro, Joa is going to be your new nanny. She needs something to do while figuring out the next phase of her life, so she might as well look after your monsters while she muses."

Ronan felt like Keely had put a stun gun to his chest and pulled the trigger. Instinctively he knew there was no way he could allow Joa to step into his house; she wouldn't make it three feet in before he kissed her. She was temptation personified.

There was no way she could work for him...

No. Damn. Way.

And, judging by Joa's completely horrified response to Keely's suggestion, she felt the same.

Shock flashed in Joa's bright eyes and annoyance slid across her face. It was obvious that she didn't appreciate Keely's "throw it against the wall, see if it will stick" idea.

Joa held up her hands and nailed Keely with a hard look. "Will you please stop trying to organize my life?"

She asked the question as if Keely was even remotely capable of keeping her nose out of her friends' business. "Joa, you're going to be bored within a week. You'll need something to occupy your time."

"I've been on my own since I was a kid, Keely. I am perfectly able to arrange my own life," Joa replied, her calm tone containing an undercurrent of annoyance. "And I've just come off a long-term contract. I do not want to jump straight back into looking after another set of kids."

Joa's eyes darted to his face and she forced a smile. "I'm sure your children are lovely but I don't need a job right now and I'm looking to do something different."

Fine with him. He couldn't hire Joa, didn't want to hire her.

Ronan rubbed the back of his neck. Before Thandi died he'd been super confident, completely convinced that the world was his oyster, and his lobster and his sushi, too. He made decisions on the fly, trusted his instincts, and easily sailed through any personal or professional storms.

Then Thandi died giving birth to Aron (something he hadn't believed could happen in one of the best hospitals in the Western world) and the world, as he knew it, stopped.

When he'd finally pulled himself out of his soul-stopping grief, he'd acted like the confident and charming man he'd once been. But underneath his PR persona, he was now protective instead of passionate, cautious instead of bold. He constantly scanned his environment, warding off trouble, looking for danger.

And Joa Jones was both. He knew that like he knew his own face.

"He needs help, Joa," Keely insisted.

"As one of the Murphys of Murphy International, I'm pretty sure he possesses enough skills to hire his own nanny, Keely," Joa said, not bothering to hide her irritation.

"Not if you go on his history," Keely snapped back before Ronan could respond. "He's gone through six."

Placing his hand on Keely's shoulder, he squeezed

gently. It was time to end this conversation. "Thank you for your concern, Keels, but I'll take it from here."

Keely looked mutinous but Ronan raised his eyebrows, silently insisting that she not push, and she sighed.

"Life would be so much easier if people just did what I suggested," Keely muttered. "I know what I'm doing."

Ronan's mouth twitched with amusement. "Very inconvenient for you that us lesser mortals possess something called free will."

"Very inconvenient," Keely agreed. She adjusted the strap of her bag on her shoulder and nodded to the ladies' room at the end of the hall. "Give me a moment, Joa, and then we'll go home."

"Thank God," Joa muttered when Keely hustled off. "I thought she'd never stop arguing."

Ronan looked down into her exquisite face and itched to rub his knuckles over her high cheekbone, to slide the pad of his thumb across her sensuous bottom lip.

Wow. What was wrong with him?

Ronan straightened and folded his arms across his chest, pulling his eyes off her lovely face. He searched for something to say—he normally had a million sound bites so why didn't his tongue want to work properly?—and when nothing came to him, Joa tried to break the awkward silence.

"I hope you find a nanny. I'm sure your boys are very sweet."

"You'll meet them this afternoon since Keely offered to look after them."

Joa shook her head. "I've been traveling for days and I'm going to catch up on some sleep, so I'll probably miss their visit. But Keely has mentioned them in her emails. She says they are adorable."

At three and five they *were* adorable. They could also be demanding and challenging. And, occasionally, more than a handful. "Thanks."

Truth was, he did need someone experienced with children. Ronan thought about interviewing another set of nannies and shuddered.

He couldn't think of anything he'd less like to do.

Maybe Joa could be persuaded to change her mind and maybe, if he tried hard, he could ignore the chemistry, could contain his rogue thoughts around stripping her down and taking her to bed.

"Are you sure you're not the in the market for a job?"

"Pretty sure." Joa tucked her long, straight black hair behind her ears.

Right. Fine.

Actually, her refusal was a relief. While he desperately needed help, the last person he needed in his house was someone who made him wonder whether her skin was as smooth as it looked, whether her mouth was sweet or spicy or both.

Ronan rolled his shoulders, uncomfortable with his errant thoughts. His brothers occasionally raised the subject of his dormant sex life, insisting that it was okay to have needs and act on them. Up until today, he'd shrugged off the odd bout of feeling horny. He'd thought that one day, way in the future, when he put enough distance between him and Thandi's death, he'd consider sex again. He'd expected his libido to slowly wake up, giving him time to come to terms with a new reality.

Meeting Joa Jones was like life had placed a defibrillator on his sex drive.

Ronan muttered an F-bomb under his breath.

There was a reason why he avoided sex. He'd never been good at one-night stands or casual flings and the "separating the deed from the emotion" concept. For him, sex was the gateway drug to relationships and he wasn't interested.

Thandi was irreplaceable and his love for her didn't allow room for another woman, another relationship. He didn't care how difficult it was to raise his sons alone, he refused to slide another woman into his wife's place. That wasn't ever going to happen...

He was still married. He might not wear her ring anymore but those ties, those promises of loyalty and fidelity, hadn't been broken by death.

They wouldn't ever be.

Time to get back to work, to walk away from the incredibly lovely, very distracting Joa Jones. He handed her a brief smile. "It was nice meeting you, Joa."

Joa tipped her head to the side and nodded. "You, too, Ronan. I hope you find the au pair you are looking for."

They both knew it wouldn't be her.

Three

She'd had five hours of sleep and it was nearly dinnertime when Joa made her way down to the kitchen on the ground floor of Mounton House. She looked around, saw no sign of Ronan Murphy's boys and nodded, relieved.

"You just missed the boys. They left ten minutes ago," Keely told Joa as she stepped into the room.

Dropping onto the wide window seat, Joa pulled her feet up and wrapped her arms around her knees. After leaving Murphy International she'd been too tired to fight with Keely about her managing ways and, honestly, a bit side winded by her red-hot attraction to Ronan Murphy.

But she knew she couldn't let Keely's bossiness go unchallenged so she tossed Keely a what-the-fudge? glare. "About your suggestion for me to look after Ronan's kids... What the hell were you thinking, Keely?"

Keely put the kettle on the gas stove and reached for two mugs. "Chamomile or peppermint?" She didn't look even remotely chastised by Joa's deep frown.

"Peppermint."

Keely dumped a bag into a bone china mug. "I know you, you'll need to do something soon, Ju. You hate being idle. And Ronan needs a nanny. Where's the problem?"

She loved Keely, she did, but at some point, Keely would have to realize that Joa was no longer a scared, insecure waif from the streets who needed decisions made for her. "And it didn't cross your mind to ask me whether I wanted another au pair job?"

Keely leaned her butt against the counter and crossed her ankles. "I thought you liked being an au pair."

She did. She liked the kids, she liked the unstructured environment, being able to go to work in shorts and flip-flops. But there was a big downside to her job and that was her inability to stop loving the family she was living with and, on more than one occasion, the man of the house.

She was done with being on the periphery of someone else's family.

On her first au pair contract, she'd looked after the five-year-old son of Liam, an Australian gold mining magnate who'd gained custody after a bitter divorce. She'd been Liam's shoulder to cry on, his best friend and, after five months, she was convinced that their friendship was heading toward something real, something deeper. Then Liam had met Angela, fallen head over heels for her and married her within three months of meeting her.

A year later Joa had gone to work for Johan, a German banker who was recently divorced from Hendrik, and she'd looked after the twin daughters they'd adopted from Vietnam. She knew he was gay, but she couldn't stop herself from dreaming that she would become a permanent part of his life...

Johan had been smart enough to recognize her crush and gently suggest she move on, telling her that there was no possibility, ever, of them being more than friends. She'd taken a break and traveled for a while, before accepting a job with the Wilson family. Dave was married, she rationalized; she'd never fall in love with a married man.

She hadn't fallen for Dave; she'd fallen for *all* of them. Annie became a close friend and quickly became a second sister, and their kids were smart, funny and interesting. Joa had loved working for them—not that it felt like work!—and for the first time in her life, she'd felt like part of a functional family unit.

She'd felt secure and safe. And loved. Now, in hindsight, she knew that her attraction to Liam and Johan had been a rationalization for her need to be part of their family, her desire to be loved and needed. She adored her bosses because they were good men and excellent fathers. They put their children first.

Something neither her parents nor her foster parents had ever done for her.

On leaving New Zealand, feeling discarded and tossed aside—her fault, not the Wilsons'—Joa knew she couldn't repeat her past mistakes. She needed to switch careers, to find a job or a passion that didn't involve families and kids.

She had two choices: she could come to terms with being single and childless or she could actively look for someone to create a life with, to have children with.

Both scenarios terrified her.

She didn't want to be alone, but neither did she want to risk rejection.

Devil and the deep blue sea...

"Ronan is a good guy who is going through a difficult time, Joa." Keely pulled her back to the present.

"The guy is rich and successful. He can afford to hire the best nanny in the city," Joa argued. Respectfully, his hard time wasn't her problem.

Keely wrinkled her nose. "I don't know what it is with him but he always, always seems to hire the wrong people. Since Lizbeth, he's been a magnet for bad nannies."

Joa knew there were a lot of weird people out there—she always insisted on a two-week trial period and had left two families when it didn't work out—and not every nanny was Mary Poppins.

But she still wasn't the person for the job.

"I don't want to au pair anymore, Keels. I really want to try something different."

Keely placed her pointed chin in her hand. "Why? You have a master's degree in child psychology and you are so good with kids."

Joa wished she could explain how she insinuated herself into other people's lives. It wasn't healthy and it wasn't…right. And she wasn't doing that anymore.

Especially since Ronan Murphy was exactly the type of guy she was drawn to…

Oh, hell, why was she even attempting to lie to herself? Her other two single bosses were nice men, reasonably attractive, but Ronan had blown her socks off. The man made her tingle, made the moisture disappear from her mouth. She wanted to know how it felt to have his hands on her bare skin, taste his smile, feel those broad shoulders, that wide chest, that hard stomach.

He was hot and sexy and, worst of all, a single dad. If she went to work for him, she gave herself a day before she started fantasizing about becoming his significant other, stepmom to his supposedly adorable boys.

She wouldn't be able to help herself; it was what she *did*.

Not this time.

And not with that man.

Because Joa suspected that if she went to work for Ronan Murphy and once again fell for her single-dad boss, she'd, yet again, end up lost and alone and rejected.

And she didn't know if she'd be able to pick herself up and start again…

When she spoke, her words were soft but laced with emotion. "I can't do it, Keely. Not again."

Keely, because she was perceptive as well as pushy, frowned. "Did something happen at your last job that I should know about?"

Sure, I keep creating a fantasy that never comes true.

"I'd like to do something different, Keels, that's all."

She needed different.

Keely pulled a face. "There's something you're not telling me," she complained, picking up the kettle and pouring hot water into the mugs. She picked up the mugs and walked over to Joa, placing a cup on the built-in table in the corner of the window seat.

There was an enormous amount that Joa wasn't telling Keely. She never discussed her childhood before coming to live with Isabel and Keely, couldn't talk about the isolation and the neglect. She'd been one of the lucky ones. She hadn't been sexually or physically abused, but others, she knew, weren't that fortunate.

But as she'd transitioned from child to teenager, her unusual looks garnered attention not only from lascivious foster fathers but also from her older foster brothers. When her foster father started looking at her in a non-fatherly way, Joa knew she was in trouble. Unable to face another strange house filled with strange people, she'd taken her chances on the streets. She'd lasted three days before landing at Isabel's shelter and, from there, into this wonderful house with Isabel and her great niece, Keely.

Joa had been so lucky. So many girls who chose the streets didn't end up safe. And none of them, of this she was certain, inherited an equal share of one of the largest fortunes in the country. Isabel had given Joa a safe place to stay, an education and, by writing her into her will, lifelong financial security. She'd loved Iz intensely, but Isabel had flown in and out of this house and their lives and was never the fully engaged "mom" Joa needed.

Iz had loved being on her own. She'd never needed a husband to make her feel complete. Maybe Iz was onto something. Maybe it was time for Joa to be more like the woman who'd rescued her half a lifetime ago—emotionally independent, sensible and strong.

Isabel had never looked to a man to make her happy and maybe Joa should honor her foster mother by following in her independent footsteps.

Keely cleared her throat and Joa turned her attention back to the present. "It's unlike you to be so intransigent, Ju. Or to refuse to help someone who so obviously needs your help."

She was just trying to protect herself. She was so done with feeling heartsore and miserable, feeling rejected when she walked away from another temporary family.

She couldn't keep hurting herself, borrowing other people's people. She needed to protect herself because, God knew, nobody else would do it for her.

"I'm sorry you're disappointed in me," Joa replied.

She *was* sorry, but she wouldn't change her mind about working for Ronan.

Keely covered Joa's hand with hers and released an audible huff of frustration. "I'm not disappointed in you, I'm just confused. And because you are the most private person in the world, I don't understand why you're being stubborn about helping Ronan. You know me inside out, Ju, but even after so many years together, in some ways you're as much a mystery to me as when we first met."

Joa wished, she genuinely did, that she was more open. It wasn't that she didn't trust Keely, she absolutely did, but Joa was naturally reserved and a little shy. And, for most of her life, she'd lived in an environment where it wasn't always healthy to draw attention to oneself.

It was a hard habit to break.

Seeing the flash of hurt in Keely's eyes tightened Joa's throat. The words weren't easy to say, but she'd push them out; she owed her sister that much. "I'm sorry, Keels, opening up isn't easy for me. But I do love you. You know that, right?"

Keely's eyes lightened and the corners of her wide mouth tipped up. "Of course I know you love me, you goose. I just wish you'd let me inside that head of yours."

Joa wished she could, too. She could offer to try, but she hated making promises she wasn't sure she could keep.

Thinking that it was past time to change the subject, Joa sipped her tea and looked at Keely over the rim of her mug. "So I looked at the list of Iz's possessions to be auctioned off by Murphy International in their spring sale. Is that the final list?"

"Why? Is there something you want to keep? We can withdraw anything at any time," Keely quickly replied.

Joa held up her hand. "I'm happy with your selection, Keels. But as I walked through the house, I noticed that there's still a lot of furniture and stuff left in the house. What are we going to do with it all? And what are we going to do with the house?"

Keely shrugged. "We need to talk about that. And we need to discuss Isabel's foundation. The CEO left a month back and we need to look for someone to run it. It's a full-time job and I can't do it, I'm swamped."

Keely was a speech therapist and loved her work. Joa was happy her practice was thriving. "Now that I am back, maybe I can help out with the foundation, take a little of the load off you."

Keely smiled her appreciation. "That would be awesome, thank you. So, about this house. Do you agree that it's too big for either of us, or even both of us?"

She did. Who needed a fifteen-bedroom house with four reception rooms, two libraries and a ballroom?

"We could sell it…"

Joa pulled a face. "I don't want to live in it, but I don't think I want it to go out of the family, either. Besides, who would buy such a huge house?"

Keely's eyes turned stormy. "Stuffy Seymour says

we could convert it into luxury apartments. He has a developer friend who is interested in doing just that."

Joa tipped her head to the side, intrigued by the annoyance she heard in Keely's voice. Keely was the friendliest person she knew—bossy, sure, but she liked people and people liked her back—so Joa couldn't understand her antipathy to Isabel's lawyer. "What on earth did he do to upset you?"

Keely refused to meet Joa's eyes. "I don't know what you mean."

"Keely, you've done nothing but grumble about him since the day you met. From what I can see, he's been professional and he's done a great job of looking after our interests. Yet you seem to be perpetually pissed off with him. Why?"

Keely's shoulders inched upward. "He just annoys me. He's arrogant and bossy and thinks he knows everything about everything."

Pot. Kettle. Lots of black.

Joa swallowed her smile, intrigued by the idea that Keely had finally met a man she couldn't wind around her baby finger. So what was it about Dare Seymour that raised such fury in Keely? Joa couldn't wait to find out. "Let's invite him to dinner."

Keely looked horrified. "What? Why?"

Joa felt laughter in the back of her throat. Payback was *such* fun. "I'd like to thank him for all his hard work."

"He's getting a percentage of Iz's estate for working that hard," Keely complained.

As Dare was one of the most successful lawyers

in the city and came from a famous and cash-flush old Boston family, they both knew he didn't need Iz's money. "Keels…"

"I'd prefer to keep it businesslike," Keely muttered.

If Keely really wanted to keep it professional then she wouldn't be squirming in her chair. And why were her cheeks flushed? *Oh, Keely Matthews, what is going through your head?*

Joa made up her mind. "I definitely think he should come to dinner."

Keels drooped her head to the surface of the table and gently banged her forehead against the laminated surface. "Why do you hate me so much?"

"More to the point, why do you hate Dare Seymour?"

"I don't hate him." Keely's reply was muffled. "He just irritates me. I don't know why."

Joa thought it was time that Keely found out. "Tell me what date suits you and I'll set it up."

Keely groaned. "I hate you so much right now."

Joa reached across the table to pat her head. "No, you don't, you love me."

"I can do both. It's a skill I've perfected," Keely mumbled.

After Keely's surprise pronouncement two days before—and after trawling through résumés of nannies, finding problems with all of them—and two days of hell juggling the boys—Ronan thought he should talk to Joa again about the possibility of her coming to work for him as a temporary nanny.

He was *that* desperate.

On the pro side, she had au pair experience and she was immediately available. And Keely, someone he knew and trusted, could vouch for her good character.

If he wasn't attracted to Joa, he wouldn't have hesitated to try and talk her into coming to work for him. But something about her caught his attention in a way that both scared and annoyed him. Yeah, she was beautiful, stunningly so, with her light eyes and warm skin.

And that wide, sensuous mouth made for kissing...

A huge con was that Joa was the first woman to pique his curiosity and interest after Thandi, and if he was smart, which he obviously wasn't, he'd be running in the opposite direction.

But, because dividing his attention between two young boys and his demanding career was freakin' exhausting, he'd texted her last night and asked if she'd pop around to meet him early this morning, before work, to discuss Keely's out-of-the-blue proposal.

Because she was a little early, and he was very late, he was only dressed in exercise shorts and trainers when she walked into his house at eight the next morning. Ronan wished he'd had time for a quick shower after his workout or, at the very least, to toss on a shirt before her arrival, but nope...

Ronan led her into the kitchen area of his great-room-slash-kitchen-slash-living-room. In comparison to him, she looked fresh and feminine, filling the air with her subtle fragrance.

The urge to bury his sweaty face in her neck, to

taste those sexy lips, was strong. Ronan closed his eyes. In his gym clothes, if he sported some wood, there would be no way to hide it. He looked past Joa's shoulder to the photograph of Thandi on his fridge and his erection subsided.

Sorry, love. Forgive me.

Ronan rubbed his hand over his jaw, feeling his stubble. He needed to shave, but that wouldn't happen this morning. "Sorry, we're running late."

Joa placed her bag on the granite counter of the center island. "I see that."

Ronan couldn't help noticing how her cranberry-colored silk sweater flowed over her amazing breasts. He swallowed and started to recite mathematical equations in his head. Unlike his brother Finn, Ronan didn't find math a turn-on.

"The kids are still asleep. They wouldn't settle down last night, so I eventually put them into my bed and put on a movie, thinking that would lull them to sleep. No such luck. I also overslept, so it's a bit mad around here," Ronan said. "And I have a crazy day ahead of me."

"How so?" Joa asked, sliding onto a barstool and crossing one long leg over the other. Those legs went on for miles and he'd love to feel them around his hips or, if she was adventurous, around his neck.

Ronan wrenched his mind off what a naked Joa would look like and, needing something to do that hid his reaction to her, turned his back to check the water and coffee beans in his state-of-the-art machine.

Right, she'd asked about his day.

"This time of the year, as we plan the spring sales, every day is crazy. I will be home late tonight. I'm running a specialized sale on sports memorabilia."

As he turned to look at her over his shoulder, he caught the flash of irritation in her eyes and wondered if she thought he'd assumed she'd be available to babysit for him tonight. He wasn't that arrogant.

Ronan turned to face her and gripped the counter behind him. He answered the silent question he saw in her eyes. "Finn, my younger brother, agreed to look after the boys for me tonight. Luckily it's only a small auction, so I should be done by ten."

"I thought you only ran the big sales."

It was a fair observation. As director of global sales and marketing and the company's head auctioneer, he normally didn't bother with the nuts-and-bolts auctions. "Normally I let the junior auctioneers run the smaller sales but my sports guy had a family emergency. I do have other auctioneers but there are some pretty big spenders in the audience. I thought I'd run the sale, connect with them on a guy-to-guy level."

"I'd like to see an auction," she admitted.

If she attended, he wouldn't be able to concentrate. "You're always welcome," he lied, "though I am assuming you will be at the auction for Isabel's collection. It will be one of the biggest auctions any house has conducted. It's been billed as a once-in-a-generation sale. So it's not a big deal or anything," Ronan quipped.

Joa tipped her head to the side. "I presume that you

know that Sadie thinks only one of the three paintings might be by Homer?"

Ronan nodded. "If Sadie manages to prove the painting's provenance and if it turns out to be by Homer, it will be the last item auctioned."

Joa had the prettiest frown he'd ever seen. "Do you think it's genuine?"

For her and Keely's sake he hoped it was, but he never, ever gave anyone false hope. And it was important to manage expectations. "I genuinely don't know. Obviously, for your and Keely's sakes, I'd like it to be genuine. But I never emotionally invest in anything that passes through our house. I can appreciate the skill and rarity and beauty but I know we are only temporary guardians of the artwork. And I refuse to waste my energy worrying whether a piece is genuine. It either is or isn't and I can't change the result."

Instead of pouting, sulking or looking disappointed by his prosaic statement, Joa tipped her head to the side and seemed to give his words some thought. "That's a fair assessment," she eventually told him.

Smart and thoughtful. Damn, his life would be so much easier if she was just another pretty face. Pretty and sexy he could easily ignore, but pretty, sexy and smart was a killer combination.

Joa lifted her hand to fiddle with the clip holding back the sides of her hair. Her extraordinary eyes met his and electricity arced between them.

No! He needed to kill that current. Immediately.

He knew just the way to do that. By being concise and controlled. Businesslike.

So get to the point of this meeting, Murphy. You need a nanny, she is one. Convince her to take the job and work out how to hide your attraction later.

"I need a nanny, desperately. I'm asking you to consider working part-time for me, mostly in the afternoons, until I can find someone else. And, if you do come to work for me, I assure you that nothing will happen between us, Joa."

"Why would you think it would?" Joa demanded. Her back straightened, her mouth tightened and she tapped an index finger on the granite, completely irritated. Good, irritation he could handle...

Ronan needed to push, to make sure there was no wiggle room on this. Nothing could, or would, happen between them, No matter how attracted he was to her, or she was to him. He was still emotionally tangled up with Thandi.

"Look, I know you've been checking me out, that you're attracted to me."

He thought he heard a snort, something that held more disparagement than amusement. But he couldn't miss the panic in her eyes. "I'm almost thirty years old, and a healthy female who hasn't had sex in a while, and you're a good-looking guy."

But?

"But the world is full of good-looking guys, Murphy, and I can take or leave them."

Now that sounded like a challenge. And Ronan had never backed down from a challenge in his life.

Or was he using her challenge as an excuse?

Either way, knowing he was making a mistake, but

unable to stop himself, Ronan moved swiftly to stand next to her, so close he could see the tiny sparks of lightning in her eyes, each individual eyelash and the tiny scar on her top lip. She smelled like moonbeams and mystery and Ronan knew he wouldn't be walking away without tasting her, just once.

Lifting his hand, he brushed his thumb across her bottom lip, waiting for her to pull back. If she did, he would step away.

But Joa surprised him by placing her hand on the bare skin over his heart and when she arched her back and lifted her mouth to reach his, he took her move as the invitation it absolutely was.

Ronan's lips touched hers and his skin sizzled in response. He felt her fingers dig into his chest, the rasp of her nails as he lost himself in the softness of her mouth. Joa sighed and her lips opened and he slid his tongue inside, groaning as he did so. She tasted of coffee and strawberry lip balm, of frustration and fierce desire. It was a combination designed to make his head swim, to cloud his thinking. He couldn't, wouldn't, allow himself to touch her with anything but his mouth. He couldn't take the chance of losing all his control.

In a moment he'd stop kissing her, in just one more moment…

Keeping his hands fisted at his sides, Ronan kissed her for another minute, and then another, fighting his urge to pull her closer, to find out how well her lithe body would fit to his. He was so big and she was so slim but he knew they would be combustible together and that was why they had to stop...

Now. Immediately.

It still took him another minute to release her mouth, to step back. When he did, he turned away to grab the edge of the island, needing something to hang on to.

What in the hell just happened?

Ronan heard Joa's small curse, felt her sliding off the stool to move away from him. He heard her footsteps and turned his head to watch her move to the sink, before reaching for a clean glass on the shelf above her head. The tap ran and she filled her glass, the space between them vibrating with tension. Joa took a long drink of water before turning her back to the sink, resting her glass in the crook of her arm.

Ronan saw Joa's eyes skate down his body and when hers widened he looked down to see his erection tenting his exercise shorts. Well, crap.

Joa closed her eyes and shook her head. "We shouldn't have done that."

"Yeah, not our best move."

He thought he saw disappointment in her eyes, a flicker of hurt. But he had to be wrong; they were barely more than strangers and hardly knew each other.

This was just desire. There was no emotional connection to be had, not with her or anyone else. They'd kissed. Why was he making a mountain out of a couple of grains of sand?

Could it be because he'd never had such a crazy reaction to anybody, ever? Not even to...

No, he couldn't go there.

That would be a betrayal. Shaking his head, he forced the thought away.

He needed to get his morning, and his life, back on track. "You're a sexy woman and yeah, I'm attracted," Ronan conceded. "But—"

"But it's still not going to happen," Joa finished his sentence for him, rolling her eyes. "Damn straight it's not. I prefer my lovers to be excited about taking me to bed, not angry and resentful."

Ouch. But fair.

"So let's admit that there's a mutual attraction that will not be acted on. Agreed?"

Ronan managed a sharp nod and begged his blood to return to his brain.

Joa reached for her bag, pulling it over her shoulder. She looked past him and Ronan turned to see what captured her attention. Damn, it was the photo of Thandi, her hand holding her hat to her head, blue eyes sparkling, and her smile wide.

His heart cracked. Asking Joa to come here had been such a bad idea, one of the worst he'd had. He needed to backtrack, but Joa beat him to it.

"Going back to why I am here…" She gripped the bridge of her nose before forcing her eyes to meet his. "I'm sorry, but no, I can't help you with your boys.

"Best of luck, I hope you find someone suitable." Joa added, walking toward the huge square entrance to the hallway. Then she turned and sent him a tight smile.

"Oh, and if you don't want your female employees lusting after you, then I strongly suggest you put on some clothes when you conduct job interviews, Murphy. Walking around half-naked isn't conducive to keeping the arrangement businesslike and might give potential nannies the wrong impression."

The heels of her boots clicked on the marble floor in his hallway and then he heard his front door opening, then closing. Ronan slumped onto the closest stool. Joa wielded a mean verbal punch. It was just another thing he liked about her.

Crap.

Four

He was late…

Again.

Ronan stepped out of the lift, looked at his watch and grimaced. Thanks to Sam's teacher wanting to talk to him this morning—apparently it was his turn to provide the class with nut- and gluten-free cupcakes on Friday—he was ten minutes late for the Murphy weekly management meeting.

Eli stepped out of their suite of offices, holding out Ronan's favorite cup. Ronan wrapped his fingers around it and took a big sip of coffee before dumping his coat and leather briefcase into Eli's arms.

"You know I hate asking you to do personal stuff for me, but please will you organize cupcakes, free of gluten, dairy, peanut and tree nut, to be delivered to Sam's school on Friday?"

Eli's love of food was reflected in the slight paunch under his lime green shirt. Today, his pants were a sober black. Eli wrinkled his nose. "What's the point of having cupcakes, then?"

"I'm presuming they are trying to avoid a kid being rushed to the hospital in anaphylactic shock," Ronan dryly replied.

Eli sniffed. "The idea offends me."

Ronan smiled. Eli was often dramatic but he was smart and efficient and often caught the balls Ronan dropped.

And he made truly excellent coffee.

Ronan sipped, sighed and gestured for Eli to walk with him. "Anything I need to know before I go into the meeting?"

Eli nodded, his usually merry face sober. "Yeah. As you well know, the Beijing office is holding a sale in Chinese ceramics…"

Ronan nodded. For the last twenty years, rich Chinese citizens were on a mission to bring Chinese art and artifacts back to their country. The French collector who'd decided to liquidate his extensive collection of Asian ceramics and jade through Murphy International was expecting a multimillion-dollar payday.

"…the head auctioneer was rushed to the hospital with a suspected burst appendix. He's currently in ICU."

Ronan grimaced. He liked Wu, a longtime employee of their Beijing office. "Crap. Is he going to be okay?"

"Yeah, he'll be fine. But Mei Lien isn't comfortable asking Chen to run the auction."

Hell, he wasn't comfortable asking Chen to run the auction, either. The younger man was Wu's apprentice, but he had a long way to go. He didn't have the experience to run an auction of such prestige and importance.

"She wants you to run the sale," Eli explained when they reached the conference room. Ronan looked through the glass doors and saw the meeting had already started. His brother Carrick was standing at the head of the table, his hands holding the back of the chair. Ronan grimaced, remembering that it was his turn to chair the meeting. While Carrick was, technically, the CEO, Ronan and his two brothers ran the company together.

Ronan mouthed a quick sorry to Carrick and turned back to Eli. "Tell Mei Lien that I will call her as soon as I get out of this meeting."

Eli nodded and opened the door for him. Ronan walked into the room and nodded at Carrick, who moved away from the chair. Pulling the chair away from the table, he dropped into the seat and silently thanked Eli for the agenda, complete with handwritten notes, lying on the table in front of him.

"Sorry I'm late."

Finn, his younger brother, leaned forward and rested his forearms on the table. "Problems, Ro? Eli looked a bit frazzled."

Ronan glanced down at the agenda and decided that his Beijing problem needed to be prioritized. And since this wasn't a formal meeting—and the three other people at the table were long-standing and completely trusted employees—he gripped the bridge of his nose and muttered a quiet, heartfelt curse.

Ronan explained that he needed to head to China that night.

"I'll order the company jet to be prepared and have the pilots file a flight plan," Carrick said, as decisive as ever. Carrick knew, as well as Ronan did, that he didn't have a choice; he was needed in Beijing and he needed to leave that night to make tomorrow evening's sale.

He hated to bring his personal life into the office, but this time, he didn't have a choice about that, either. "I'm stuck for childcare," he admitted, frustration coating every word. "Thandi's parents are still on their three-month Caribbean cruise and I haven't found a new nanny yet."

Carrick winced. "I'd have them in a heartbeat, Ro, but I'm leaving for London in the morning."

Ronan looked at Finn, who shook his head. "I'm going with Carrick, Ro. There's a collection we are looking at."

Ronan groaned. He trusted his brothers with his kids and, more important, Sam and Aron loved spending time with their uncles. There was minimal discipline, forgotten bedtimes and plenty of unhealthy snacks and video games.

"We're looking at his collection and taking him to dinner at Claridges. Beah is joining us."

Finn, as he always did, flinched at the sound of his ex-wife's name. Why those two ever got divorced Ronan had no idea.

Carrick exchanged a look with Marsha, his PA, who was sitting to his left, taking notes. "Can you get hold of Cummings, ask him if we can postpone viewing his collection?"

Paris Cummings was one of the world's most reclusive and elusive collectors. He never allowed anyone to view his collection and only sold pieces from his massive art collection under the direst circumstances. Or when he needed to liquidate some cash to purchase a bigger, or rarer, artwork.

"Cummings? You've got an appointment to see him?" Ronan asked, surprised. "Why didn't I hear about this sooner?"

Carrick lifted one shoulder. "I know Paris from way back. I remember Dad introducing him to me when I was still in high school. He contacted me directly and I roped in Finn. I emailed you."

Ronan hadn't even had time to look at his laptop. Hell, he was dropping balls left, right and center.

Finn picked up where Carrick left off. "He heard about the Vermeer that is part of the Mounton-Matthews collection and he's prepared to sell some of his lesser pieces so he can bid on it. He wants me to evaluate his collection."

Being trusted to sell off some of Cummings's works of art was a coup and Ronan knew how capricious the man could be. If he didn't think Murphy's was paying him enough attention, he'd refuse to meet with them, call up Christie's or Bonhams and move his art through them.

Finn and Carrick missing the appointment with Cummings was not an option. "I'll make a plan for the kids. Maybe I'll just take them to China with me," Ronan said, only half joking.

"You'd still need someone to look after them while you work," Marsha pointed out.

Ronan saw Carrick's lips twitch at her literal response to the joke, but he just nodded at Marsha's earnest expression. "True, Marsha." He saw his brothers' anxiety and sent them all a reassuring smile. "Maybe Keely will take them for me."

"Or Joa. She's an au pair and has experience in looking after kids," Finn suggested. He leaned back and pushed the tips of his fingers together. "Didn't I hear something about Keely suggesting that Joa be your temporary nanny?"

Ronan nodded. "It didn't suit either of us. She's not looking for work right now…"

And he didn't want anyone under his feet, or in his house, who made him feel prickly and uncomfortable and…aware. Sexually aware.

He didn't need to spend his time lusting over his kids' nanny. It was tacky. "I hate getting a stranger to look after them but if I have to, I'll call an agency and get a temporary sitter."

Carrick gestured to the pile of papers in front of him. "Why don't the rest of us carry on with the meeting, Ronan, and you head back to your office and make arrangements for the kids? I can take them tonight but not tomorrow night."

"Ditto," Finn said as Ronan stood up.

Ronan nodded his thanks and picked up his pile of papers. He took the top sheet and handed Eli's handwritten notes to Carrick. "Let me know if there is something you want my input on."

"We'll manage," Carrick said. "Let us know what you need from us."

"Will do." Ronan stood up and pushed his chair back. He sent each of his brothers a quick look, hoping they saw his appreciation. These men had his back, had always been the two pillars propping him up. From Thandi's death to taking the kids when he desperately needed a break, they were there for him.

He couldn't have navigated the past three years without their constant support. He wanted to express his gratitude, but this wasn't the time or place.

So, because he found it difficult to be vulnerable, he swallowed the words down and hoped they knew how grateful he was that his brothers were his two best friends.

One day, he'd find the guts to say thank-you.

"I wish I could help you, Ro, but I'm out of town, at a conference in Miami. But Joa is at home and I'm sure she'll help you out. If she can't, I'll come home."
After speaking to Keely, Ronan knew Joa was his last shot before hiring a sitter from an agency, something he didn't want to do. Oh, he knew the sit-

ter would be professional and come highly recommended, but he hated the idea of leaving his kids with someone he didn't know.

Leaving his kids with Joa—the woman he hadn't been able to stop thinking about—was still better than leaving them with someone he'd never met before.

Ronan ran up the stone steps to the front door of Mounton House. Ronan had visited before, with his stepmom, Raeni, and remembered Raeni pointing out the massive staircase, the exquisite moldings, glimmering chandeliers and carved mahogany paneling. He'd been ten and thought that the huge hall would make an excellent bowling alley and the staircase would be great to slide down.

While he waited for Joa to respond to the pealing doorbell, he shifted his attention from his lack of babysitters to wondering what Keely and Joa intended to do with the enormous mansion. Others like it had been turned into apartments and he supposed that was an option; it really was too big for a modern-day family. Ronan glanced at his watch, tapped his foot impatiently and rocked on his heels. After hitting the doorbell again and getting no response after five minutes, he called Keely again.

"She's not here," Ronan told her. "Any idea where I can find her?"

"She's there. She's probably doing yoga in the ballroom and zoned out. I can scream at her and she doesn't respond. There's a keypad to the left of the door, do you see it?" Keely said.

Ronan's eyes flicked over the door and he saw the discreet panel. "Yeah?"

Keely gave him the code. "The ballroom is at the end of the hallway, toward the back of the house," Keely told him. "Go hunt her down."

Ronan thanked her, punched in the code and pushed open the heavy door. In the hallway he inhaled the smell of beeswax polish and fresh flowers and looked at the massive walls sporting faded squares and rectangles where art pieces, up until a couple of months back, graced the walls. Those paintings, along with dozens of others, were now in the Murphy International vaults, or out getting cleaned or reframed.

Ronan heard his footsteps echoing in the huge space and took a moment to admire the hand-carved staircase. His ten-year-old self had liked the idea of sliding down the banister—and the man he'd been before Thandi's death probably would've tried it.

Finn, his daredevil brother, wouldn't hesitate.

Ronan rather missed throwing caution to the wind, but then he thought about his boys and remembered that they only had one parent and that he couldn't take any unnecessary risks.

So he admired the intricate carving, the skill of the carpenters and the quality of the Italian marble before striding down the wide hallway, peeking into rooms as he walked past open doors. He'd grown up in a house full of antiques and while he preferred modern furniture and art, he still appreciated the workmanship and history of the eighteenth-century Chippendale table, the solid silver Georgian candelabras and a five-foot Ming vase.

As he walked deeper into the house, Ronan heard the faint sounds of music drifting down the hallway and knew he was getting closer. The music wasn't what he expected from a yoga session; it was heavy rock, with long guitar riffs occasionally punctuated by a deep, thirty-cigarettes-a-day voice.

It was loud, rough, sexy music. The type of music he'd once loved and never listened to anymore.

Ronan saw the half-open door and pushed it with his foot, his heart slamming against his ribs as he watched Joa place one hand on the floor and extend her leg up so she was practically doing splits, standing up. God, those legs...

He knew they were shapely but the Lycra fitted her like a second skin. Joa, still unaware of his presence, dropped her leg and effortlessly slid into another pose. Keeping her hands on the floor, she tucked her knees behind her elbows and, without a hint of strain, balanced only on her hands. Then she moved her bent knees to the side and held the pose.

And he'd thought he had decent core muscles.

"Crane pose."

Ronan, fascinated at how she was moving her body, took a moment to realize she had spoken. He blinked once, then twice.

He shot an uneasy look down the hall, thinking he should explain why he was in her house. "Keely gave me the code. She said you were here."

Joa pulled one leg up to her chest and let her other leg extend behind her.

Ronan shook his head. "How the hell do you do that?" he asked, stepping into the room.

Joa lifted her head to look at him. "Practice."

Dropping her legs to the floor, she released her arms to stretch out into one of the few yoga poses he could name. "That's the child pose."

Joa's bare shoulders shook with what he presumed was amusement. "Very good. You do yoga?"

"Uh, no." Thandi had, for a few months in between her pregnancies, but she'd never gotten beyond the basics.

"It's great for stress relief."

But her outfit wasn't. Her exercise pants had sheer cutouts in the thighs and calves and her matching top, ending just beneath her breasts, and showing off a tight, super flat stomach, had the same sheer cutout bridging her breasts. Beneath the black Lycra and sheer material was creamy, rich skin.

She'd pulled her hair up into a pile on top of her head and she wore no makeup. She didn't need it.

God, she was beautiful.

Joa walked, her bare feet not making a sound, across the big room to pick up her phone off the small table tucked into the corner of the room. She tapped the screen, the music abruptly stopped and silence dropped into the space between them.

Joa picked up a bottle of water and walked back to him, her light eyes on him while she sipped. "Why are you here, Ronan?"

He couldn't remember. All he could think about was slapping his mouth onto hers and rolling that Lycra down her hips and the top up and over her breasts, revealing all that skin to his appreciative eyes. Conscious that his pants were tight and that air felt scarce, he pulled the water bottle out of her grasp and took a long, reviving sip.

The cold water didn't help him at all. He still wanted her.

Crap. Dammit. Hell.

"Ronan?"

Ronan handed the water bottle back and scrubbed his face, wishing he could dispel the image of those long, strong, supple legs wrapped around his hips, her nipple in his mouth. He held up his hand. "Give me a minute."

"Are you okay?"

Ronan shook his head. No, he was drowning under a tidal wave of lust, looking for air as desire swamped him. He hadn't felt like this for years, if ever. He'd loved Thandi with every fiber of his being but he'd never felt such instantaneous, heart-stopping lust. Never, not even with the wife he still loved and still mourned.

The wife who wasn't here...

Ronan pushed back his grief and his guilt at feeling the way he did, focusing his attention on why he was here, what he needed. He wanted more than anything to leave the room, to walk away from Joa with her light eyes and milky skin and bendy, amazing body. But unfortunately, he needed her help.

"I need a favor," he muttered, noticing that his voice sounded rough. From desire or irritation? Or a combination of both?

Joa didn't respond except to raise her already arched eyebrows higher.

Dammit, he hated asking for help, especially from a woman whom he needed to avoid, but he was, as his English stepmom used to say, in a pickle. "I need someone to look after the boys, tonight and tomorrow night."

Joa lifted her bottle to her lips and frowned. She shook the bottle and then he realized that he'd finished her water. He gestured to the empty bottle. "Sorry."

"I can get more," Joa replied. "Why are you asking *me* to look after your boys?"

"My brothers are going to London to meet with a cantankerous, reclusive collector, and Tanna, my sister, has also gone back to the UK. I haven't found another nanny yet and Keely is—"

"Out of town."

Ronan jammed his bunched fists into the pockets of his beige chinos. "Yeah. I'm stuck. I mean, I could hire a babysitter but I don't like strangers around my kids, in my house."

Joa cocked her head. "Where are you going?"

"China. I need to run a sale in Beijing."

"Chinese ceramics and an incredible collection of carved jade."

It was Ronan's turn to lift his eyebrows. "And you know that how?"

A touch of pink hit Joa's cheekbones. "I might've visited your website."

Ah. "My senior auctioneer is in the hospital and the head of the Beijing office isn't confident in his apprentice."

Joa tipped her head to the side at the same time as she placed her right foot on the inside of her left thigh. The odd pose took nothing away from her beauty.

A small frown appeared on Joa's forehead. "I'm sorry, are you trying to tell me that they want you to run the sale?"

Ronan nodded.

"But you're American. Do you use an interpreter?"

"No, I manage since I speak close to fluent Mandarin."

Joa's mouth dropped open. "Really?"

"My stepmom insisted that we learn another language. My brother Finn, being the intellectual over-achiever that he is, learned a whole bunch. I think he's fluent in six or seven, and able to converse in three or four more," Ronan explained. "I chose to go with one, thinking I'd choose Mandarin because it was really hard and maybe Raeni would let me give it up in a few weeks because I wasn't making any progress."

Amusement flashed in Joa's eyes. "Except that she wouldn't let you quit."

"And I wasn't as bad at it as I thought I'd be. Then I spent a year at the Beijing office when I left college." Ronan shrugged, thinking they were way off subject. "Anyway, I'm going to run the auction but I need someone to stay with my boys."

"Me?"

"If you're willing."

"And if I don't say yes?"

Ronan rubbed the back of his neck. He was stuck but he wasn't going to beg. "Look, if it doesn't suit you, I'll call an agency, ask for an emergency sitter. It's not something I want to do, but I'm out of options. This sale will be one of the biggest of the year and many influential billionaires are expected to attend. Handing them an inexperienced auctioneer would offend them and our clients will feel like they are not important enough to rate a decent auctioneer. It would be a snub Murphy International might not recover from."

Joa bit the inside of her lip and Ronan waited for her response. "Two nights?" Joa asked, tapping the empty bottle against her thigh.

"Tonight and tomorrow night," Ronan said, hope building.

Joa's chest rose and fell in a movement that suggested agitation. Or resignation. He didn't care, as long as he got a yes.

"Okay. I'll do it."

Ronan felt his stomach unravel and his lungs release the air he'd been holding. *"Thank you."*

"But just for two nights, Murphy. I'm done with au pairing. I'm trying to find a new direction, a new path to follow."

He didn't care what she did with the rest of her life, he just needed her for the next forty-eight hours. But he did need to find a new nanny soon; this situation was bordering on ridiculous.

"I'm so grateful." And he really was. Ronan twisted his wrist, looked at his watch and gestured to the door. "Is there any chance that you could leave with me now? I need to show you the house, then we need to collect the kids from school and introduce you to the staff there so they'll let you collect the kids tomorrow."

Joa gestured to her bare feet and skimpy gym outfit. "Can I shower and change first? And I need to pack a bag."

Now that he had her agreement, Ronan was loath to let her out of his sight in case she changed her mind. But if he bundled her out the door and into his car just as she was, he'd look like a raving idiot.

"Okay. I'll wait—" he looked around the empty room and lifted his hands "—where?"

"In the kitchen," Joa replied, walking toward the door. "There's a coffee machine, help yourself. Or maybe you should have a cup of chamomile tea. You're looking a bit stressed."

She had no idea.

Five

Joa was pretty sure that at one time, Ronan's house in West Roxbury had been a designer showcase. His low-slung couches and carefully chosen furniture screamed Nordic minimalism, the bold art giving the eyes a break from the very white double-volume walls.

Joa stood in the great room off the hall—a long and wide room that held a sitting room on one side and a well-designed kitchen on the other with a huge island and a white wood dining table splitting the two spaces—and the huge windows provided views of what was once a landscaped but was now a neglected and denuded garden. Joa wrapped her arms around her body and turned in a slow circle in the huge room. Sadness could sometimes be a tangible thing.

Joa's throat tightened at the image of Ronan's stunning wife in a silver frame on the dusty surface of the Steinway piano. She was cuddling her toddler—Sam?—her huge stomach telling the world that she was about to birth another child, her wide smile tender and her eyes full of happiness.

This was still her house, in so many ways. There was a massive portrait of her immediately catching attention as one stepped into the hall. There was a wedding photograph of her and Ronan on the hall table. A Hermes scarf, pink and gray, hung off the coatrack, as well as a gray felt hat adorned with scarlet flowers.

To Joa, it felt like Thandi had stepped out to run an errand, or that she was upstairs. This was still, in every way that counted, her house.

But there were hints of Ronan, too: a tie on the granite counter, cell phone chargers, a shopping list in what had to be his scrawl on the fridge. And, of course, signs that kids lived here. There was a small shoe under the leather sofa, a green glove on the floor, die-cast metal cars on the Persian carpet.

A massive train set crisscrossed the corner of the room and toys of all description were tossed into boxes, into corners, piled up on chairs.

Yep, this house was chaos. Yet she still preferred chaos to clinical sterility.

Joa turned at the sound of footsteps and her breath caught when Ronan strode into the room, pulling a small suitcase with a laptop bag resting on top. He'd changed into a light gray suit, a pale mint green shirt underneath the designer jacket.

Stepping into the great room, Ronan glanced at his watch and grimaced. "We have so much to talk about and minimal time."

Joa perched on the arm of one of his long and wide sofas. She crossed her legs and linked her hands around her knee. "On a scale of one to ten, how upset are your boys going to be having a stranger look after them?"

Ronan rubbed the back of his neck and Joa saw the worry in his green-gold-blue eyes. "I'm hoping they'll be fine and they'll feel better if we pick them up from school together. Sam is stoic, he's a mature kid, but Aron might get a bit weepy."

Ronan walked across the room to the double-door fridge and pulled out a bottle of water. He waved it in Joa's direction. "Still or sparkling?"

"Sparkling." Joa joined him at the granite center island and slid onto a barstool, perfectly content to watch the tall, rangy, ripped-as-hell Ronan move around his messy kitchen. God, she was so attracted to him. Really, what warm-blooded woman wouldn't be? Thank God she was only going to be his nanny for two nights; more would be impossible.

Joa refused to put herself in the position of having and losing a family again. It hurt too damn much.

It was like putting yourself into a story where you didn't belong, singing a hymn when you should be chanting, painting with oils when you should be sketching with pencils.

She had money, she had time, she had choices. She had so much more than she, a child from the wrong side of the tracks, had ever expected. She owed it to Isabel, to herself, to find her niche, to write her own story, her own song, to live her own life instead of hijacking someone else's.

She was helping Ronan out; she would be out of his life within forty-eight hours, and then he would just be a memory. It didn't matter that she was brutally attracted to him and he kissed like a dream; she was not going to allow herself to indulge in the smallest fantasies around him.

She was all about reality now...

Ronan picked up her water bottle and dashed the liquid into a glass before pushing it across the granite surface in her direction. "We need to leave in fifteen minutes, so let's use that time to go over the ground rules."

"Sure."

Thankful for his businesslike tone, Joa listened as he ran through his dos and don'ts, all of which were pretty standard. Then Ronan pointed to a round light in the ceiling. "I have cameras everywhere so I can see what's going on. All the time."

Joa narrowed her eyes. "Define everywhere? My bedroom, my bathroom?" And that reminded her... "Where am I sleeping, by the way?"

Ronan pushed his hand through his hair. "The boys share a room on the top floor, next to mine. But the guest suite is a floor down. The nanny usually stays there."

Joa shook her head. "I won't hear them if there's a problem."

Ronan took a long sip of his water. "There's an iPad next to your bed. Switch it on and you can see and hear what they are up to. If the boys are upstairs and you are down here, you can carry the iPad and check up on them."

Handy in a place as big as this but he didn't answer her question. "Do my bed and bathroom contain cameras?"

"No, of course not."

Ronan drained his glass and picked up her half-full glass and took them through to what she assumed was a utility room. "We need to go." Ronan told her when he returned, looking reluctant.

Joa sensed how difficult it was for Ronan to leave his sons with her. Sure, Keely had vouched for her and she had nannying experience but she was still a stranger and he wasn't just leaving the city, he was going halfway across the world. If anything went wrong, he'd be nearly seven thousand miles away.

She saw him hesitate and knew he was second-guessing himself. Knowing that he was on the point of calling off his trip—she could see it on his face— she stepped over to him and placed her hand on his strong forearm, feeling his heat despite his shirt and jacket.

"They'll be fine, Ronan, I promise."

Ronan handed her a look that was long on disbelief and short on confidence. "You can't promise that," he muttered.

Okay, he was splitting hairs, but she got it. "True. Okay, how about this? I will do everything in my power to keep your boys safe. Everything I possibly can."

Ronan stared at her for a long time and Joa knew that she couldn't break the eye contact. If she did, he'd call off his trip. After what seemed like a millennium passing, his shoulders dropped and his face relaxed. He managed a small smile. "I'm being ridiculous, aren't I?"

Oh, that self-deprecating smile was too charming and too sexy for words. It made him seem years younger and very approachable. Joa smiled. "A little. But you're their dad. It's allowed."

"Sometimes I think I've made it into an art form. But I am so damn scared that something will—" He stopped abruptly, his words drying out. Joa waited, hoping he'd finish his sentence but he just shook his head, as if irritated with himself. "Ignore me, I'm rambling. Let's go."

Ronan took her hand and linked her fingers in his, his other hand reaching for his suitcase. As he pulled her and the suitcase toward the front door, Joa was conscious of his strength, the way his big hand enveloped hers, his palm and fingers dwarfing hers. In his hand, hers felt small and feminine and, yeah, safe.

And were those tingles she felt skittering up her arm? Yep, she thought they just might be.

In the hallway, Ronan stopped at the front door and looked down at their linked hands. He pulled his hand from hers and smiled wryly. "Sorry, force of habit. I'm constantly grabbing a child's hand."

Joa felt a vicious stab of disappointment, mortified that while she was thinking of him in terms of being a sexy man, he equated her with being a child.

Joa folded her arms and waited for him to open his front door. "I'm not a child, Murphy." She couldn't help the comment, knew that she was poking a bear with a stick, but she needed him to see her as a woman.

Stepping into the cold wind of a late January day, Ronan pulled the door shut behind him and sent her an inscrutable look. "Trust me, I noticed."

And what, Joa wondered as he led her over to his white Land Rover sitting in the driveway, did that mean?

On her second night of babysitting duty, Joa made herself a plate of nachos and poured herself a glass of red wine. She was just about to sit down in the media room to watch reruns of *Downton Abbey* when she heard the doorbell ring.

Taking a slug of wine—and hoping that the strident doorbell didn't wake Aron who'd refused to go to sleep without three stories, a cuddle and a monster-under-the-bed check—she placed her nachos on the coffee table and headed to the hall.

In yoga pants, a slouchy sweatshirt and comfy socks, she wasn't dressed for receiving visitors. Then again, she wasn't expecting company and anyone who made house calls so late without advance notice was just plain rude.

Joa looked at Ronan's iPad, clicked on the screen showing the view of the front door and saw Keely standing on the steps, accompanied by a tall man built like a lumberjack, his back to the camera. What was Keely doing here at this time of night?

Joa hurried to the hallway, yanked open the door and gasped at the frigid air. Looking past her guests onto the dark driveway, she saw that it was snowing.

Again.

Joa reached out and grabbed Keely's arm, tugging her into the hallway. The Armani-wearing lumberjack followed her inside. In the brightly lit hall, Joa immediately recognized that masculine face: Dare Seymour, the man she had yet to invite over to Mounton House for a casual meal.

"Hi, Dare, Keely. What are you guys doing here?" Joa asked, shutting the door behind him.

Keely unwound the scarf from around her neck and shrugged out of her coat. Dare took her coat, hat and scarf and hung her garments next to his on the coat rack by the door. Without asking, he plucked her gloves from her hands and tucked them into the outside pocket of her coat. His movements were economical and easy, as was the kiss he dropped on Joa's cheek. "Hi, Joa. It's been a long time."

"Hi back," Joa said, her eyes darting from his implacable face to Keely's stormy expression. Oh, God, what were these two arguing about now?

"Sorry to disturb you." Dare said, pushing back his jacket to slide his hands into the pockets of his suit pants. "I did tell Killer that this could wait until tomorrow but she insisted on getting the issue settled now."

What issue? And Dare called Keely Killer? Did he have a death wish?

"Do not call me by that ridiculous name," Keely said, obviously irritated.

"Why do you call her that?" Joa asked him, as she led them through to the great room and gestured for them to take a seat.

Dare waited for Keely to sit down before taking the seat next to her on the big sofa, stretching out long, muscled legs. The guy had to be six foot five plus and he sucked up space. With his dark blond hair and masculine features, he looked like Thor.

"I call her that because she reminds me of one of those feisty Jack Russell dogs who think they are a lot bigger and scarier than they actually are."

Oh, God, Joa shouldn't laugh, she really shouldn't...

When Keely sent her a fulminating, you're-dead-to-me look, Joa realized she hadn't managed to hide her amusement. She winced and shrugged. Unfortunately, Dare's characterization was spot-on.

But she'd rather die than admit that to Keely.

"Can I offer you something to drink? I've just opened a bottle of merlot."

"I can't stay," Dare said, shaking his head.

"Hot date?" Keely asked, in a super sweet, sarcastic voice.

"As a matter of fact, I do," Dare smoothly replied.

Keely opened her mouth to say something, then flushed and snapped her teeth shut. Keely turned her head away from Dare and stared out of the floor-to-ceiling windows at Ronan's tree-filled backyard, where snow gathered on the bare branches.

Dare stared at Keely's profile, exasperation on his

face. Wanting to avoid blood on Ronan's furniture, Joa sat down on the chair opposite them and leaned her forearms on her knees. "So, what's up? What did you come to talk to me about?"

Dare rested his arm on the sofa behind Keely's head. Joa noticed Keely stiffen, then relax fractionally, as if unable to help the back of her head brushing his wrist. Awareness jumped in and out of Dare's eyes and Joa knew that if she got up and left, that sofa might see some action.

Of the "I don't like you but I'm going to kiss the hell out of you" variety.

"I received a letter from a film director this afternoon. He's arriving in Boston at the end of this week to start filming a turn-of-the-century horror." Dare said.

Joa wrinkled her nose. She liked action movies with sexy heroes but horror films gave her nightmares. And how did any of this concern her?

"Isabel rented Mounton House to him shortly before she died," Dare said. "He paid her an extraordinary amount of money to rent the mansion and its furnishings for the film. According to the correspondence between him and Isabel he forwarded to me this afternoon, Isabel was planning on spending the next three months at her villa in the south of France."

She'd forgotten that she and Keely owned a French villa.

Joa looked from Dare to Keely. "And this arrangement is binding?"

Dare nodded. "I saw the contract. She accepted his money and his entire crew is already in the city. If you two don't agree, he can sue the estate for monies paid, for breach of contract and for loss of profits."

"That's absurd," Keely muttered.

"I never said he would win, I said he could sue. And that would garner some press attention since he's very well-known and influential—"

"As a director of horror films?" Keely scoffed. "Sure he is."

Dare ignored her. "My point is that you do not need bad PR, as the publicity for the auction is starting to gather traction. And this would be bad PR."

Joa looked at Keely, still staring out the window, her expression stubborn. Joa knew that Keely hated the idea of strangers in their house. She'd even objected to Isabel's open houses and tours, thinking they were a security risk. "You're not keen on the idea, are you, Keels?"

Keely eventually looked at her. "No, I hate the idea of strange people in our house, touching our stuff. While the most treasured items have been moved to the storage facility at Murphy International, there are still some very valuable items there. And if someone stole something, we'd never know because there's so much."

"We have an inventory from the estate, and Derek has agreed to employ security and to put systems in place to negate any theft and damages." Dare said. "I will review those arrangements and if I'm not satisfied, I will insist on more security."

"They can't guarantee that nothing will be stolen or damaged, can they?" Keely demanded.

Dare shook his head. "There aren't any guarantees in life, Keely." He thought for a moment. "Maybe we should hire an additional security company I trust and we'll pass on the cost to the production company."

"That's a good idea, Dare, thank you," Joa said.

Joa widened her eyes at Keely, silently reminding her to use her manners. Keely wrinkled her nose and her next words sounded like they'd been pulled out from under a fifty-ton boulder. "Good idea."

"I have them occasionally," Dare dryly responded. Dare turned his attention back to Joa. "Another thing… Most of their filming will take place at night because it's a horror film. That means that you'll both have to move out."

Oh, that wasn't good.

Keely scooted to the edge of her seat and placed her elbows on her knees. "I'm actually heading to Florida for a month to work with a special needs school down there, so I was leaving for a while anyway. But you'd have to move out, Joa."

Dammit. She rather liked her massive four-poster bed, doing yoga in the ballroom, sitting in Iz's library amongst her books.

Joa looked at Dare. "Do I have to? Can't I stay there and keep out of the way?"

Dare shook his head. "They've been promised an empty house and that's what you'll have to give them."

Joa quietly cursed. "When do I have to leave?"

"Mid next week," Dare said, spreading his hands in an apologetic gesture. He stood up and looked down at them from his great height. "So, are you agreeing to let the house?"

Joa raised her eyebrows. "Do we have a choice?"

"You always have a choice," Dare replied.

"I suppose we have to honor Isabel's arrangement with him. Where will you go, Joa?" Keely asked her, looking worried.

Joa had a healthy bank account and she could afford to hire an apartment or move into a hotel for a few months. "I'll be fine, Keels. And I agree, I think we should abide by the contract Iz signed, as inconvenient as it is."

"Okay, then. But I'm not happy," Keely muttered.

Joa smiled. "Yep, I'm getting that vibe."

Dare glanced at his watch and pulled a face. "Let's go, Killer, I'm tired. I want a drink and some food."

"And to join your hot date," Keely added, her tone dark.

"Exactly so," Dare agreed, his tone genial.

Confusion and annoyance flashed across Keely's face. Joa suspected that Keely might not like Dare Seymour but she didn't like the idea of him dating anyone else, either.

Now wasn't that interesting…

But as much as Joa would like to focus on the weird vibe between Keely and their sexy lawyer—really, between the Murphy brothers and Dare Seymour, Boston was looking pretty fine these days—Joa needed to think about where she was going to live for the next three months.

She heard a thump coming from the hall and

frowned. Jumping to her feet, she rushed across the room but Darc's long stride beat her to the hall and she was grateful for his large presence. Had she locked the front door behind Dare and Keely? Who was in the house?

She had two young boys upstairs, and she had to get to them...

Joa darted around Dare to get to the staircase and skidded to a stop when she saw Ronan standing by the hall table, dropping his keys into the flat, ceramic dish on the hall table.

She blinked, shook her head and blinked again. He was only due back sometime in the morning...

Joa put her hand on her heart and sucked in the sight of him. He wore dark black chinos and a mulberry colored sweater under a thigh-length leather coat, and he looked hot.

If Dare was Thor then Ronan could easily play a not-quite-so-perfect Superman...

Come on, Joa, you can't keep staring at him, acting like he's a salted caramel ice cream you can't wait to taste. Say something, dammit.

"Um...hi? You're home early."

"Yeah. Some lots were withdrawn from the sale so the auction finished earlier than I expected."

Ronan's eyes darted from her to Keely to Dare, obviously curious as to why they were in his house this late. After hanging up his leather coat, he pushed the sleeves of his sweater up his arms, shook Dare's hand and dropped a kiss on Keely's cheek.

Joa rocked on her feet and wondered if he'd kiss

her, too. She wanted him to but also didn't. Mostly because a casual kiss just might turn combustible…

She so wanted his lips on hers again, his tongue in her mouth.

"Ju. All good? Are the kids asleep?"

Joa, jerked out of her sexual haze by the casual use of her name, just nodded. She cleared her throat and tried to be the adult she was reputed to be. "All good, and yeah, they are fast asleep."

"Any problems?" Ronan asked.

Strangely, there hadn't been. The boys had been remarkably accepting of her presence in their house.

Ronan pushed his hand through his hair. "I'm just going to check on my kids and then we can have a drink."

Dare shook his head. "Keely and I were just leaving, Ronan. We popped around to give Joa a heads-up about an upcoming change to her circumstances."

Ronan shot her a concerned look. "Problem?"

Joa quickly shook her head. "No, nothing insurmountable." She walked over to the coatrack and picked Keely's coat off the hook, pushing it into her sister's arms.

"When do you leave for Florida?" she asked, keeping one eye on Ronan's back as he jogged up the stairs.

"Not for a day or two," Keely said. "I'll be going back and forward for the next couple of months. But I'll catch up with you in the morning and we can talk."

"Sure," Joa replied. She looked up, and up, into

Dare's face. "Thanks for stopping by, Dare. When Keely gets back from Florida, you should come for dinner."

"I'd like that, thank you." Dare bent down to kiss her cheek. Keeping his head close to hers, he dropped his voice but not enough to keep his words from reaching Keely. Which was, Joa realized, his intention. "But, please, can you cook? I'm terrified Killer will slip something into my food."

"It's a distinct possibility," Keely said, pulling on her gloves. "Especially if you keep using that stupid nickname."

Joa shut the door behind them, leaving them to bicker. She looked at Ronan's suitcase and laptop bag and sent an anxious glance up the stairs. He was home, so she should head back to Mounton House.

Ronan's footsteps on the stairs had her looking up and she immediately noticed he'd changed into straight-legged track pants and a tight-fitting Henley, sleeves pushed up his strong forearms. Instead of six-hundred-dollar loafers, he wore thick socks.

This was what he'd look like on a normal night at home, a man at ease in his space. For the rest of her life, she'd remember him looking like this, sexy and rumpled and a little stressed.

Before she could say anything, Ronan's phone rang and he pulled it out of his pocket. Joa was surprised when he placed it on speakerphone.

"Hey, Carrick. How's London?"

"Wet, as always. I had a meeting with Beah this afternoon."

Now that was a name she hadn't heard in a while. Beah, she remembered, was Finn Murphy's ex-wife but she was also one of Keely's closest friends. She also, if she could trust her memory, worked for Murphy International out of their London offices.

"Everything okay?" Ronan asked Carrick.

"Sure. I had some time earlier so I went through Isabel's inventory with Beah and she has a fair idea of which art collectors will be interested in the Mounton sale."

"Thanks. That takes some pressure off me."

"Is Beah still joining you and Finn for dinner with Cummings?" Ronan asked.

"Mmm. Hopefully it won't be as awkward as I'm imagining it to be."

"Um…have you seen Sadie at all?" Carrick then asked and to Joa, he sounded, strangely, hesitant. It wasn't a trait she associated with the Murphy brothers.

Joa's pulse skyrocketed at Ronan's smile and the amusement lightening his incredible eyes. "Well, no. Since I've been in China for the best part of two days. Why are you asking about our art detective? Do you not have her number?"

"Of course I do. She's not answering." Carrick tersely replied.

Ronan grinned at Joa. "Maybe she's on a date."

Carrick's only answer was a muffled growl.

"Or maybe she isn't as attracted to you as you are to her." Ronan teased.

"I...what... I've got to go. If you speak to her, tell her I'm looking for her. No, don't bother...*dammit*."

Joa smiled at the mischief in Ronan's eyes.

"You're sounding a bit unhinged, dude." Ronan said, sounding smug. When Carrick abruptly disconnected the call, Ronan laughed.

Joa cocked her head. "Why were you hassling Carrick about Sadie?"

"Because something is brewing between them and it's my brotherly duty to give him crap about it."

Man, smiling upped his sexy factor by a thousand percent and Joa's stomach did backflips. And then a double twist. She needed to go. Before she did something really stupid.

Like throw herself at **him.**

Bite the bullet, Jones. "I'll call a taxi and I'll be out of here in fifteen minutes."

Ronan frowned at her. "That's not necessary. It's freezing out and it's late. Go home in the morning."

Joa pulled the inside of her right cheek between her teeth. Should she stay or go? She looked out the window, saw the wind had picked up and the snow was swirling. The weather was dreadful and it was a fine excuse to stay...

She really shouldn't stay...

"Okay. Thank you."

An awkward silence fell between them, which Ronan eventually broke with a wry smile. "I need a huge glass of wine and some food. Any ideas?"

"I made the kids a rice-and-fish dish, and there's

some left over. I also made spicy nachos for myself. You can share."

"Nachos sounds perfect," Ronan said. "Wine sounds better. Let's go…"

Said the sexy spider to the fly…

Six

Beah Jenkinson exited the black taxi at the swanky entrance to Claridge's, grateful for her long black vintage cashmere coat. After paying the taxi driver, she tucked her designer clutch bag under her arm and sucked in a deep breath. She could do this, she *had* to do this…

It was only dinner with one of the most important and elusive collectors in the world.

And her ex-brother-in-law Carrick and her ex-husband, Finn.

Who also happened to be two of her three bosses.

Not a big deal.

Liar. It was *such* a big deal…

Beah handed a black frocked doorman a smile and walked up to the doors of the impressive hotel. Allowing her coat to swing open, she resisted the urge to check her reflection in the glass doors, to reassure herself that her off-the-shoulder, tight-fitting, cobalt blue cocktail dress with its ruffled hem was suitable.

She looked perfectly fine. She was thirty years old, a woman confident in her body and her looks. She had an amazing career, a wonderful life.

She was not the insecure girl she'd been when she met and married Finn Murphy the best part of a decade ago.

She'd been twenty-one and working as an intern at Murphy International when she met the brilliant Finn and she'd been entranced by his quick brain and his encyclopedic knowledge of art and history. Within a week they were sleeping together; within a month they were engaged. They married in Vegas on the three-month anniversary of the day they met.

After a visit to the ladies' room and a conversation with her best friend, Beah walked in the direction of Davies and Brook, Claridge's brand-new restaurant, Beah admitted that she'd gone into her relationship with Finn, and her marriage, with a cruise ship's worth of baggage. Her mother had passed away just a year before, after a six-year battle fighting cancer. Her dad, her hero and the first true love of her life, had left them both around the time she started getting ill, and it was a betrayal Beah had never come to terms with.

Maybe she'd thought that marrying Finn would close the holes in her heart, would give her the security she craved, but she'd failed to recognize the fact that she'd married the most emotionally independent and unavailable man she'd ever met. Finn wasn't a talker and he struggled with her bouts of emotion and her need for reassurance. He'd started to pull away and she'd responded by trying to pull him closer.

He'd told her that her constant demands about where he was and what he was doing, and her incessant pleas to give up his adventure sports smothered him. Having lost both her parents, one to illness and one to abandonment, Beah had lived in agony, thinking Finn would be next to leave.

After an excruciating year, Finn had asked for a divorce, telling her he loved her but he couldn't live with her insecurities.

Admittedly, the divorce had been the catalyst for Beah to change her life. It was a point of pride that eight years later, Beah was now as, or more, independent than Finn and she barely recognized the girl she'd been when she married him.

Taking the opportunity Carrick offered her to be a client liaison in London, she'd crossed the Atlantic and was now Head of Client Advisory, reporting directly to Ronan. As an advisor for both buyers and sellers, she helped the company's most important clients with the formation of, and the disposal of, important collections.

As for her and Finn, well, they communicated when they needed to, via very brief and pointed emails. Working for the same company, they'd run into each other over the years but they both made a concerted effort to avoid each other as much as possible.

But Paris Cummings was an important collector, one she'd been pursuing for years, and she had to attend this dinner, had to join the two Murphy brothers in their attempt to woo the stubborn collector to their side of the fence.

And that meant sitting at the same table as her ex-husband, pretending that all was well.

All *was* well… It had to be.

At the entrance to Davies and Brook, Beah smiled at the maître d' and gladly surrendered her coat. Resisting the urge to check that no fire-red curls had escaped her smooth chignon, she looked over the exquisitely decorated dining room, her eyes immediately going to the best table in the room.

As if he could feel her eyes on his dark blond head, Finn jerked his head up and their gazes clashed and connected. Beah's feet were glued to the floor; she was unable to pull her eyes off his masculine, oh-so-handsome face. A short, tidy beard covered his cheeks and jaw, his hair was overlong and could do with a trim, and his shoulders were wide in that designer suit tailored for his tall frame.

Finn pushed to his feet, unfurling his long and muscled body. He wore a black shirt without a tie and his eyes—a light, light green—remained on her with laser-like intensity.

He used to look at her like that while they were making love, as he was about to slide into her. Like she was a puzzle he didn't understand but needed to complete…

"Ms. Jenkinson? Ma'am?"

Beah heard her name being called from a place far away and she wrenched her eyes off Finn onto the concerned face of the maître d'.

"The Mr. Murphys are expecting you and, I'm sure, delighted to have you join them." He gestured her to precede him.

Beah forced herself to cross the room, her face impassive. Yeah, she could pretty much guarantee that Finn Murphy was *not* delighted to see her.

Just as she wasn't thrilled to see him…

It was both strange and nice to come home to a gorgeous, sexy, sweet-smelling woman after an exhausting business trip, Ronan thought as he inspected the bottle of red wine Joa left on the kitchen counter. Although he had a rack of wine in the corner holding better and more expensive bottles, and an extensive collection in the state-of-the-art cellar in his basement, she'd brought her own, a decent red, and he appreciated the gesture.

He helped himself to a glass and watched as Joa assembled a plate of nachos for him. Judging by the smells wafting his way, he knew that she'd used proper Mexican ingredients, from chipotle seasoning in the ground beef to refried beans. He was hungry and had he been asked what he wanted to eat, ground beef nachos wouldn't have crossed his mind, but seeing the ingredients hitting the plate, his mouth started to water.

It had been well over three years since a woman had prepared a meal for him in his own house and it felt both weird and wrong, but he was too exhausted to care. He just wanted some food, a little conversation and the soothing properties of a good merlot.

He didn't need to overanalyze every damn thing. And he couldn't help noticing how unbelievably sexy Joa was—despite her messy hair, her skin devoid of any makeup and clothes that completely hid her amazing curves. He dismissed his thoughts as a normal straight man's reaction to having an Indian goddess look-alike in his kitchen.

"You wear glasses."

Joa's head shot up and she touched the frame of her delicate gold-rimmed glasses with three fingers. "I usually wear contacts but my eyes get scratchy, so I take them out and shove these on."

It was nice to know that she wasn't completely perfect. Ronan gestured to the plate. "Aren't you eating?"

"Mine is in the media room. I was about to eat when Keely and Dare arrived."

Ronan nodded and slid off his barstool. Within a minute he'd collected her plate and glass of wine and placed both on the island. Joa smiled her thanks as she scattered sliced jalapenos over his nachos.

Ronan resumed his seat at the counter and placed his arms on the granite. "So what's your change of circumstances?"

Frustration and worry crossed Joa's face and

flashed in her eyes. She turned to take the cheese out of the fridge and Ronan saw the tension in her stiff back, in the way she held her head. When she finally turned around, she flashed him a quick, back-off smile. She held up two blocks of cheese. "Monterey Jack or cheddar?"

Was that a trick question? "Both?"

"Your arteries just let out a massive groan."

"I work out every day, so my arteries are just fine."

Joa shrugged. "It's your heart attack."

"I'd be very happy for you to give me CPR."

Ronan heard his flirty words, surprised at his sex-tinged tone. What the hell? He was flirting? Hell, he'd thought his ability to do that had died with Thandi. It should've died with Thandi!

Guilt, hot and sour, washed over him and he took a large sip of his wine. He risked looking at Joa and noticed that she was giving the grating of his cheese far more attention than it deserved. Her extraordinary cheekbones were slightly tinged with pink. He dropped his gaze lower and immediately noticed that her nipples were hard and pointy beneath her loose sweatshirt and that her breathing was ever so slightly erratic.

Jeez, she was as turned on as he was. Dammit, this wasn't good.

At all.

Needing to reset their conversation, Ronan cleared his throat. "How were the monsters today?"

Joa's head flew up, all sexual awareness gone. Her eyes sparkled with amusement. "Man, they are too cute. Aron is a riot—the kid has a wicked sense of humor for a three-year-old."

Aron was more like him when he was younger while Sam was more studious. And serious. "He is funny." Then her words sank in and he grimaced. "Oh, God, what did he say?"

Joa grinned. "On the drive home, I asked them to tell me some of your rules and I got the standard responses…pick up your toys, say please and thank-you." Joa's grin was wide and infectious and he couldn't stop his lips from curving upward, even though she had yet to come to the punch line. "Then Aron informed me that only Daddy is allowed to say goddammit, *goddammit*."

Ronan laughed. "At least he didn't tell you that he wasn't allowed to pick his nose or worse."

Joa slid both their plates under the hot grill before turning back to look him in the eye. "Oh, he told me those, too."

Ronan groaned. "That kid has no filter."

"He's super cute, though." Joa picked up her glass of wine and swirled the red liquid around. She looked deep in thought and when he could look into her eyes again, he noticed her laughter had faded.

"Sam is quieter, more anxious."

Ronan straightened and frowned. "What do you mean?"

Joa placed the plates on the counter. She switched off the grill and took her seat opposite him. "When we got home, Sam asked me, twice, whether you had landed safely. I went online, showed him the website where you can track your plane via radar and found your jet. He kept checking it until you called and told him that you were safe on the ground. I don't need my psychology degree to tell me that he's scared to lose another parent, that's obvious."

Joa scooped up some meat with a piece of tortilla and popped it into her mouth, keeping her eyes on him. He didn't want to talk about his kids or his dead wife. Hell, he wasn't sure he wanted to eat, unless it was to devour her. He reminded himself that he was hungry, and forked food into his mouth. It was delicious and they ate in silence for a few minutes. "This is great, thank you."

"Pleasure," Joa calmly replied, meeting his eyes. Attraction and hot, molten desire flared and Ronan wasn't sure who made the first move, him or her, but one minute he was eating, the next she was standing between his legs, her cool hands on his cheeks. Then, somehow, again without his knowledge, his hands ended up gripping her hips and his arms banded around her tiny waist, pulling her so that her breasts pushed into his chest, his thighs caging her in. He inhaled her scent and relished the feel of feminine curves, female comfort.

Then he made the mistake of dipping his head to place his lips against that small, butterfly-shaped birthmark on her collarbone...

God, she was so soft, her skin so smooth. He shouldn't be doing this, it was wrong, but he couldn't help himself, it had been so long since he'd held a woman, heard the hitch of her breath, sensed the delicious tension in her body. Should he advance, should he retreat?

Ronan was still trying to make up his mind, resist temptation, when Joa's tongue touched the cord in his neck, and electricity, hot and powerful, danced over his skin. If this was wrong, why did having her in his arms—her lithe, fragrant body pressed against his—feel so damn right?

He couldn't help it but he needed to taste her, to feed on the essence of her, so Ronan turned his head to capture her mouth. He knew how to kiss her—he'd relived their previous kiss a hundred times—but then Joa opened her mouth. His tongue slid against hers and the world stopped. Time ceased to exist as he explored her mouth, his hands running up her back and cupping her butt. His erection pushed against the barrier of his pants and he wished she'd drop her hands from his shoulders to free him, desperately needing her hot hands on his shaft.

Ronan felt dizzy and sideswiped but his body knew exactly what to do, how to please her. Sliding his hand up and under her sweatshirt, he encountered her bare breast, her nipple a tight bud. Rubbing his thumb across her, he heard her muffled moan and she arched her back in a silent plea for more. Ronan hitched up her sweatshirt and looked down at her breast, small but perfect with its dark, merlot-colored nipple. So sweet, so rich.

He ducked his head to kiss her, to pull her against the roof of his mouth, and when her hand pushed between their bodies to hold him, he groaned against her skin.

It had been so long and he knew that it wouldn't take much for him to climax. Damn, this was so much better than those lonely, sad, solo efforts in the shower.

But pleasure was so much better shared, so Ronan ran the backs of his knuckles down her abdomen, flirting with her mound. When Joa pushed his hand underneath the band of her yoga pants, he only encountered a small patch of hair—no bra and no panties, so hot!—and feminine heat. Ronan captured her chin in his free hand and pulled her mouth back to his, awash with sensations.

His hand in her pants, her hand on his shaft. Her mouth was warm and wonderful.

He'd just touch her a little, maybe get her off, and then he'd stop. He wasn't going to make love to her, he couldn't… He'd stop, he *would*.

Then Joa yanked his pants down, just far enough for her to have unfettered access and Ronan knew that this was a battle he wouldn't win, a war where he was uninterested in victory.

He wanted this, he wanted her…

To hell with it…

Ronan gripped Joa's hips and surged upward, easily lifting her. Her legs banded around his hips and she nipped at his mouth as he carried her across the room to lay her on the cushions of the closest sofa. He placed his hands on either side of her head, staring down into those passion-fogged eyes.

"Do you want this?" he demanded, his voice rough with passion. Joa stared up at him, her eyes on his mouth, filled with do-me-now. But he needed to hear the words…

"Do. You. Want. This?"

Joa didn't pretend to be coy, didn't hesitate. "More than I want my next breath. Come here and kiss me, Murphy."

In a minute. He still had something to say, if he could get the words to roll off his tongue. "It's been a while, Ju, and I'm not going to last."

Joa licked her top lip and smiled. "That's okay, I don't think I will, either." She pushed herself up to rest on her elbows. "You done talking yet, Ronan?"

Hell, yes. Besides, the conversation he most wanted to have with her was silent but powerful. Ronan stood up and reached behind his head to pull his shirt over his head. Joa watched, appreciation on her face. "Ooh, nice chest."

His mouth twitched with amusement. Keeping his eyes on hers, he pushed his pants down his hips and allowed the fabric to fall, toeing off his socks. It had been an age since he'd been naked in front of a woman but seeing the lust and admiration on her face made him feel ten feet tall, ripped as hell. He felt like himself again.

Not the boys' dad, or a widower or a Murphy, but Ronan.

Joa's appreciative eyes danced over his body and his hands itched to make her his. "Strip, Ju."

Joa, not breaking eye contact—God, how sexy was

that?—pulled her sweatshirt off and leaned back on her elbows, her pretty breasts on display. It was his turn to look, admire, salivate. Man, he wished he had ten mouths, twenty hands—there were so many places he wanted to touch, so much he wanted to do to her.

But this would only happen once and he had to prioritize, dammit.

Ronan bent and pulled her yoga pants down her hips. He threw her pants over the back of the couch, entranced by her elegant arms, her tiny waist, the curve of her hip. Her legs were long and mouth-watering and he couldn't wait to have them wrapped around his hips.

Feeling the sexual heat, he dipped a finger between her feminine folds and sighed when his fingers came away wet. She wanted him, proof positive.

He muttered a dark curse, resisting the urge to plunge and plunder.

Joa sat up and dragged the tip of her index finger over his steel hard shaft, swiping her thumb over his sensitive tip. "I'm clean and I'm on the pill. I'm presuming you are clean, too?"

He nodded, unable to speak.

Joa met his eyes and he fell into that vat of molten silver. "You can take the time to find a condom. I won't change my mind, I promise, or you can just come on home."

Choosing door number two—*thank you, Jesus*—Ronan dropped his big body to cover hers, his tip probing her entrance. Joa bent her knee to rub his hip and then her legs wound around his waist, crossing at the ankles. She was beyond anything he'd imagined...

Joa tipped her hips and rubbed herself against him and he knew he was way past coherent thought, that he couldn't stop if he wanted to.

He didn't want to...

Ronan felt her walls clench around him, felt her every shudder, every sigh. Her words made no sense; then again, neither did his. Pleasure was their only goal, giving and receiving.

He pumped, she rose to meet him, she kissed the side of his neck, he sucked on that butterfly birthmark. Her nails pushed into his butt cheeks and he welcomed the sting, the sexy pain. He slid a hand under her, adjusted his position to go deeper and Joa gasped, releasing a little scream.

He surged, she rose...

And the world shattered.

Seven

AWKWARD.

In capital letters.

Joa pulled down the throw lying over the back of the sofa and dragged it up her still pulsating body. She darted another look at Ronan.

His face was granite hard and his mouth, so soft and sensuous earlier, was compressed into a hard line.

She didn't need her advanced psychology degree to know that he was feeling guilty, regretful and, yeah, pissed.

At himself? At her? Who knew?

Ronan stared up at the ceiling as Joa stood up and yanked on her clothes. When she was dressed, she pushed her hands through her hair, which fell down her back in what she was sure had to be a tangled bird's nest because she'd lost her hair band. With her back to Ronan, she touched her lips, remembering his kiss, his passion-soaked eyes, his gentle touch.

It had been the best sex of her life.

Sex he obviously and immediately regretted. And because he did, so did she.

Joa looked over to the piano, to the silver frame containing the large photograph of Ronan's wife. Thandi was laughing at the camera, her smile wide and full of joy. Sam stood at her side and she had her hand on her massive belly, in that age-old gesture of connection.

Thandi had watched them make love. Sort of…

Joa covered her mouth with her hand, feeling a little sick. Oh, rationally she knew the woman had died a while ago, but Ronan's reaction made it feel like they'd had a quickie on the couch while she was out of the room.

It made no sense but she definitely felt like the other woman.

Thandi was everywhere in this house. There was a note to Ronan in her handwriting on the fridge— something along the lines of Thandi wishing her pregnancy to be over so that Ronan could start treating her like a sex object again—and her designer scarf still hung on the coatrack. There were photos of her pinned to the fridge by magnets, in frames and on the walls of the halls.

Joa wrenched her eyes off Thandi's face and stared at her bare toes, ridiculously angry with herself. She'd done it again, thrown herself at an unavailable man.

Okay, she hadn't been thinking of Ronan in terms of his family and wanting to be part of their close-knit circle of three but she'd stepped over a line she'd never crossed before: she'd slept with a man who wasn't only emotionally unavailable but also completely in love with his dead wife.

How messed up was that?

Feeling a little sick and a lot sad, Joa picked up her shoes and ran up the first flight of steps to her room. After using the facilities, she looked at herself in the mirror above the basin and stared into her sex-fogged eyes. It was just sex, she told herself, nothing more.

You aren't working for him, staying with him, looking after his kids on an ongoing basis. You were always going to leave in the morning...

If only the sex hadn't been so mind blowing. She wasn't an idiot; she'd realized, possibly from the first time they met, that they were attracted to each other, that something was bubbling between them. But this was more than a bubble; this was full-blown chemistry.

And if she didn't leave, if they kept connecting, sleeping together, it would blow up in their faces. Because she'd always feel like the other woman with Ronan.

She wasn't doing this to herself again; she wasn't going to look for happiness and fulfillment when there was none to be had.

Thandi might be dead, but Ronan was still very, very married.

Time to go, Jones. And she'd never be back.

* * *

Nobody knew how difficult it was to date after losing the love of your life. It was intensely hard. Not only did he feel like he was betraying Thandi's memory, Ronan felt like he was cracking open the door to a world he'd closed off, a world he no longer had access to.

Even if he hadn't had sex with Joa—sex, such a tame word for what they'd shared!—he'd still opened to her; their conversation had flowed easily and smoothly. He'd felt completely comfortable with someone other than the person he'd originally planned on spending his life with.

It felt both wrong and right, crazy and desperate. Ronan rubbed his hands over his face, staring at the note Thandi had left on the fridge, days before she went into labor. She'd been grumbling about feeling fat, uncomfortable and horny. She'd been desperate to meet their second son and neither of them imagined, not for one minute, that a half hour after he placed Aron in her arms, she'd be rushed into emergency surgery and be gone.

It was so freaking unfair.

They said that life went on, that he would, at some point, need love, companionship and intimacy. And sex. He'd done without it for so long and had been, *was*, comfortable in his self-imposed, lonely state because if you didn't get close to anybody, you could avoid the pain of losing them. Up until tonight, he'd avoided one-night stands, casual flings, brief affairs. He knew that people, his brothers and his friends, didn't understand, but in his head, he was still married, and any of the above would be cheating on his wife...

Ronan picked his still half-full wine glass and took a large sip.

The problem was that while by his own definition he'd cheated on Thandi, he didn't feel as guilty as he should. He'd had fast and furious and fantastic sex with a woman who wasn't his wife and he was...

Hell, how could he articulate this?

He felt damn good, relaxed and, yeah, maybe even a little happy. He should be racked with guilt, feeling like scum on a shoe, but he didn't...

If anything, he felt guilty for *not* feeling guilty. What did that mean? What did any of it mean? Was he just so damn happy not to be sexually frustrated that he was pushing aside his guilt so he could hold on to this postorgasmic glow? All he knew for sure was that he wanted Joa again...

And again.

Ronan turned at the sound of her heels on his flooring and his heart dropped when he saw Joa standing in the doorway, holding a large leather bag, her tote bag over her shoulder. She'd brushed her hair, slicked gloss over her lips and changed into tight-fitting jeans, knee-high boots and a cream cable-knit sweater.

"I've called for a ride. It should be here any minute," Joa said, meeting his eyes.

He started to make the offer to take her home but

then he remembered that the boys were upstairs, that he couldn't leave them alone. "You don't need to go."

As he said the words, he knew they were a lie. He did need her to leave because he couldn't think straight when she was around. He'd be distracted by her lovely skin and her expressive eyes, his thoughts constantly returning to how she looked naked and all the things he wanted to do to her. She needed to leave so he could *think*, so he could put this entire crazy night into perspective.

Joa's eyes drilled right through him. "We both know it's better if I do, Ronan." She bit her bottom lip and the fingers gripping the straps of her bag turned white. She nodded to the couch. "We both know that was a one-off thing, something inexplicable. And that it won't ever be repeated…"

Well…

Damn.

Ronan folded his arms and silently cursed when he heard a car horn announcing Joa's ride was here. Fighting the urge to go to her, to carry her up the stairs and into his bed, he planted his feet and hoped none of his confusion was reflected in his eyes or on his face. This situation was weird enough, complicated enough without letting Joa see how much she affected him.

Joa looked behind her and took a step back. "Will you tell the boys I had to leave, that I had fun with them?"

"Joa…"

He wasn't sure what he was about to say but it

didn't matter because she'd stepped out of sight. *Do not go after her, Murphy, don't you damn well dare!*

Ronan heard his front door open and close and closed his eyes, pushing his toes into the flooring. He heard the slam of a car door and only when he heard the vehicle pulling away did he release the breath he was holding, allow his arms to fall to his side.

Spinning around, Ronan grabbed his wine glass, drained the contents and then lifted Joa's glass to his lips and drank that, too.

Sometimes, there was only one decent way to get out of your head. And that was to get off your head.

Finn missed his brother.

Well, he missed the guy Ronan used to be. That fun-loving, impetuous, try-anything-once guy he'd been before Thandi died. Finn had loved his sister-in-law, they all had, but a little of Thandi's fearful attitude had rubbed off on Ronan in the years they were married, and her death had made him doubly cautious.

He was not going to like what Finn had to tell him. Finn knew how this conversation would go… He'd tell Ronan what he intended to do, Ronan would flip his lid, forbid him to do it and Finn would dig in his heels, reminding Ronan that he was an adult and could do anything he damn well pleased.

Thandi had hated Finn's adrenaline-chasing adventures and had nagged him about being careful, about the risks he was taking, frequently telling him that the family would fall apart if he died doing something stupid.

How ironic that it was Thandi who'd died giving birth, something that billions of women did all the time.

Finn leaned his shoulder into the door frame of Ronan's office and rubbed the back of his neck. In the days and months after Thandi's death, he and Carrick had taken turns spending the night at Ronan's, making sure the boys were fed and bathed and put to bed. Once that was done, they sat with their brother while he cried, stared into space or drank himself into oblivion. It was during one of those drunken rages that Ronan demanded he promise to give up adventure sports, to stop taking risks with his life.

Unable to give his brother what he wanted, Finn had compromised and told Ronan he'd always tell him when he was about to do something dangerous and it was a promise he now deeply regretted.

Ronan would hear him out, give him a thousand words and ask if there was anything he could do or say to change his mind. He'd say no and Ronan would retreat, his disapproval obvious.

Ronan took Finn's need for speed, his chasing of bigger and better thrills, as a personal affront. For Finn, it was a way to burn off stress, to get out of his head.

Some people drank, some did drugs, some screwed their frustrations away but Finn chased adrenaline. And tried, very hard, not to die while he was doing it.

So far he'd been successful.

Well, he might as well get this over with…

Finn knocked on the door frame to Ronan's office and, when his brother raised his head, instantly realized that Ronan was nursing a hell of a hangover. At one point Finn and Carrick had been worried about Ronan's fondness for drowning his grief in a bottle of Jack, but after six months, he'd cut down on his consumption of alcohol and started to be the father his boys needed. Within the year, he was back to being the social drinker they all were.

Finn stepped into his office and, because he could, raised his voice. "Hey, bro! How was the auction?"

Ronan leaned back in his chair and held up his hand. "Not so loud, dammit."

Finn grinned and dropped into the chair on the opposite side of his desk. "You look like crap."

"I feel like crap."

Ronan's honest reply surprised Finn. Wondering what had sent him to the bottle, he scrolled through his computer-like memory, searching for a reason Ronan needed to drown his sorrows. It wasn't the anniversary of his wedding or Thandi's death, it wasn't her birthday. Sam and Aron were fine and Carrick was in his office down the hall, some of his attention on work but most of it on Sadie, the attractive art detective. Finn knew they were sleeping together, that much was obvious, but he suspected that his oldest brother wasn't managing to keep their affair surface based.

Finn was sure Carrick was, as millennials liked to say, catching feelings.

Apart from Carrick's love life, it was, as far as he

knew, just a normal day at the beginning of February in cold and wet Boston. "How was the Beijing auction?" Finn asked, placing his ankle on his opposite knee.

"Some lots were pulled but the five-hundred-year-old Ming vase made bank."

"Did it break the record?"

Ronan managed a smile. "It *shattered* the record by a million five."

"Nice." Finn grinned. "Did your Mandarin pass muster?"

"Mostly. If I need a lesson in humility, speaking Chinese is a good way to get it." Ronan rubbed his forehead. "Those damn words that sound the same—"

"—homophones—"

Ronan pointed a finger at him and nodded. "Those. I swear they invented them to confuse us foreigners."

"It's all about the tone," Finn told him but knew he was speaking to a brick wall. Ronan was competent but he wasn't a natural linguist. He wasn't like Finn, who was fascinated by language, words and puzzles.

Finn tended to absorb too much information too quickly, and when that happened, he found the easiest way to slow down was to do something that took him totally out of his big brain. Since his teens adventure sports were his way to blow off a whole bunch of steam.

Talking of…

"Don't freak—" Ronan would freak, of course he would "—but I'm going to Colorado this weekend."

Ronan shot him a hell-no look. "Heli-skiing? Black diamond runs?"

Not this time but he'd do both before winter ended. "Ice climbing."

"What the hell is ice climbing?" Ronan demanded.

"We climb ice formations such as frozen waterfalls, using axes and other specialized climbing equipment."

Finn saw Ronan's jaw clench. "And have you tried this before?"

Yeah, sort of. But he wasn't about to admit that to his highly overprotective brother. "Sure."

"Liar." Ronan put his elbows on his desk and his head between his hands. "You're giving me a headache, Finn."

"You had a headache when I walked in," Finn said, rising to his feet. If that was all the grief he was going to get, he'd take it. He really wasn't in the mood for a lecture. But he couldn't help wondering what had put his brother in a foul mood and sent him to the bottle.

Finn was nearly at the door when Ronan spoke again. "I heard you saw Beah in London."

Finn tensed, as he always did when he heard his ex-wife's name. A stupid reaction since Beah was as much a part of Murphy's as he was.

"Yeah."

Ronan raised his eyebrows. "And?"

What did Ronan want him to say? That seeing Beah was both pleasure and pain, that sitting across the table from her was an exercise in torture when all he wanted to do was take her to bed?

Later, he'd acted on that impulse and he and Beah did get up close, personal and very, very naked. Making love to Beah had been better than he remembered.

Then again, they'd always been good in bed; naked they were fine, but when they dressed, they argued about everything.

Finn shrugged. "We didn't kill each other."

Then Finn remembered Beah had agreed to help organize a mutual friend's wedding. He sighed. By the time Ben and Piper exchanged vows, there was a healthy chance one or both of them would end up dead or wounded. Or worse.

He had no intention of explaining any of that to Ronan so Finn changed the subject. "Cummings agreed to move his collection through us and is working with Beah."

"Yeah, she told me. She also has a couple of clients in Asia who are interested in Isabel's Vermeer and the possible Homer—"

"It is a Homer, trust me."

"You might be right but unfortunately, your gut instinct isn't proof," Ronan responded, his tone dry.

Because Isabel's collection was such an important sale, Beah would be flying into Boston to attend their in-house meetings to discuss interest and values and possible buyers. During that time, she'd also help him organize the wedding.

He was both excited and terrified at the thought of having his gorgeous, arty, fiercely intelligent wife back in Boston.

Ex-wife. Whatever.

Finn glanced at his watch and saw that he was running late. "I have to get over to Mounton House. I need to do another sweep of the premises, make sure that I haven't missed anything important before the film crew moves in."

Ronan's frown was part pain, mostly curiosity. "What film crew?"

"Apparently Isabel rented the house to a film crew for a couple weeks, or months. Not sure how long... Anyway, they are moving in next week."

"Keely and Joa are going to hate sharing their house with a lot of people," Ronan said.

"They have to move out, that's part of the deal. Keely went to Florida. I'm not sure what Joa is going to do," Finn explained.

Ronan straightened his spine, his eyes turning the color of dangerous ice. "Joa is moving out?"

Was he not speaking English? That was what he'd said. "Apparently."

Ronan pushed his chair back and stood up, picking up his phone and wallet off his desk. "You said that you are heading over there?"

"Yeah."

"Good, you can give me a ride," Ronan stated, his words clipped.

Finn stared at Ronan's back as he strode past, his expression furious. Finn thought he heard something along the lines of Joa being an impossible woman and driving him crazy and suddenly he had the answer to his earlier question.

Ronan had hit the bottle because of a woman. A woman who wasn't his dead wife.

Finn couldn't be happier. He was also ecstatic because he'd managed to have a conversation with Ronan that didn't include "death wish" and "reckless."

It was turning out to be a decent day.

Eight

Joa was sitting cross-legged on her massive double bed, her laptop on her lap, searching for rental properties when she heard large feet hitting the stairs and stopping on the landing just outside her room. Since her bedroom was on the third floor, she knew that whoever was up here was either lost—an easy feat in a house the size of Mounton House—or looking for her.

"Joa!"

Yep, that was Ronan.

Joa, because she was a girl and he was fantastically good-looking, glanced toward the French-styled, freestanding mirror to the right of her bed and wished she'd done something other than shove her hair into a messy bun, that she'd thought to put on some makeup, some lipstick.

Thanks to reliving her best sexual encounter into the early hours of this morning—again!—she'd also had minimal sleep. Frankly, she looked like a corpse.

And, yet again, she was dressed in leggings and a bulky thigh-length sweater. One of these days she would have to show Murphy that she did own some decent clothes.

Ronan appeared in her doorway, a long cashmere coat covering his dark gray suit. His tie was pulled away from his collar and he looked like he'd had, if that was possible, even less sleep than her.

Joa put her laptop on the bed beside her and bent her knees, wrapping her arms around her legs. She tipped her head back. "Ronan? What are you doing here? And how did you get in?"

"Finn is downstairs. Keely gave us both the code," Ronan replied, pushing his coat back to jam his hands into the pockets of his pants. He looked around her room and winced. "God, it looks like a rainbow exploded in here."

Joa looked around, silently admitting that the room was a crazy combination of color: reds and oranges and pinks, a bright blue carpet and purple velvet drapes. When she first arrived at Mounton House as a teenager, this room, one of the smallest bedrooms in the house, was the only one furnished on the third floor—all the luxurious, stunningly decorated bedrooms were a floor down—and she'd liked the idea of having advance warning of anyone coming up the stairs. While she instinctively liked Isabel, trust took a lot longer and some habits took a long time to die.

As for the colors, well, she'd been happy to have a soft bed and heat, to be in a safe place, and the decor hadn't mattered. It still didn't.

This was her bolt-hole, a link to Isabel and she was used to the crazy color scheme. "Did you really drive over here to talk to me about my decor choices? And it's not that bad."

"It's awful." Ronan shuddered again. "But I do, admittedly, have a hangover."

The hangover explained his bloodshot eyes, his pale complexion. Joa dropped her knees and swung her legs off the bed and stood up.

"Why is Finn here?" Joa asked, her hand on her shabby chic bedside table. Actually, it was more shabby than chic and probably used by dozens of live-in servants over the past century.

"He's checking to see make sure he hasn't missed something incredibly special or valuable before the movie crew moves in."

"Like a Fabergé egg or a first-edition Charles Dickens?"

Ronan lifted one shoulder in an elegant shrug. "It wouldn't surprise either of us and you're closer to the mark than you realize. Back in the eighties, Isabel tossed a first-edition *Pride and Prejudice* onto Raeni's desk—"

Pride was one of her favorite books. And Isabel once owned a first edition of the famous romance? Wow. "Really?"

"Yeah. During that visit to Murphy's, Isabel also pulled a Warhol sketch and a Fabergé snuffbox out of her bag. She sold all three objects for record-breaking prices and used the money to establish her foundation."

Ronan stared at her face and Joa resisted the urge to check whether she had strawberry jam on her lips or sleep in her eyes.

"What?" she eventually asked when the silence stretched out.

"You look a little like Raeni. Like you, she was a stunning combination of Anglo and Indian genes."

Joa wasn't sure how to respond to his factual compliment. His voice was so bland but his eyes told her that he was remembering their red-hot encounter on his sofa, how they fell apart in each other's arms.

But remembering the way he kissed and the heat they generated wasn't helpful; it had been a one-time thing and wouldn't happen again.

She didn't think…

Annoyed with her lack of willpower—what was it about this man who just had to look at her to have her panting?—Joa pushed her shoulders back and arched her eyebrows. "So Finn is downstairs hunting for any overlooked treasures but that doesn't explain your presence in my bedroom at—" she glanced at her watch "—nine forty-five on a Thursday morning."

"Why didn't you tell me that you had to move out of this house?"

Well, that was a question she hadn't been expecting but it was an easy one to answer. "Because I was under no obligation to?"

Ronan's eyes flashed with irritation. "Where are you going to go?"

She wasn't sure yet, unable to decide between a furnished apartment or taking a suite at the Forrester-Grantham for a few months. She didn't want to do either: hotels were impersonal and apartments were lonely. While she liked to be able to retreat when she felt like she needed some solitude, she liked knowing that people were in the house, that she wasn't completely alone.

She hadn't been truly alone since she spent those few terrifying nights on the cold streets of Boston nearly fifteen years ago. She'd never felt so scared, so utterly vulnerable. She'd come a long way but she still hated the idea of complete solitude.

But Keely had left Boston and Joa had no friends in the city. She'd simply have to suck it up. Maybe a hotel would be better; if the silence and loneliness overwhelmed her, she could head down to the bar or sit in the lobby.

She didn't need to talk to anyone or interact, she just needed to feel safe. It wouldn't be fun, precisely, but she'd be okay. "I think I'll take a suite at a hotel," Joa told Ronan, even though her plans shouldn't concern him at all.

"That will be as expensive as hell."

Thanks to Isabel, she could live out of a hotel for the rest of her life and still have enough cash to buy a Caribbean island. Or two. She was one of the wealthiest women in Boston, a weird and strange reality. "I can afford it."

"Maybe. But it's not something you really want to do."

Joa jerked her head up, surprised that he'd picked up on her reluctance. Damn, but the man was more perceptive than she gave him credit for. "How did you come to that conclusion?"

"You have the most expressive eyes in the world," Ronan replied. "And I'm good at reading body language—it's part of what makes me a good auctioneer."

Man, she really needed to work on her poker face. She didn't need him to see her thoughts, especially the ones she had about stripping him naked and exploring that rangy, muscular body.

Ronan walked over to the window and leaned his shoulder into the windowpane, looking down at the snow-covered garden below her window.

"Come home with me."

Joa frowned, not sure that she'd heard him right. Her heart rate shot up and her stomach whirled and swirled. "Sorry, what?"

Ronan continued to stare down at the drifts of snow. "Come back to West Roxbury. Move in with me...us."

Uh...

Joa didn't know what to say. What was he proposing? Or did he just feel sorry for the poor little temporarily homeless rich girl? Realizing that her knees were the consistency of jelly, Joa sat down on the edge of the bed.

Ronan finally turned around, resting his butt on the wide wooden windowsill, stretching out his long legs. "I need a nanny, you need a place to stay. Help me out with the kids in the afternoon and, occasionally, some evenings. I'll pay you."

"I don't need your money, Murphy," Joa replied, irritated.

"But you do need a place to stay and I do need help," Ronan stated, his eyes steady on her face. "The boys were devastated to find you gone. From the moment they woke up it's been Ju this and Ju that."

His boys were lovely but… "I don't want to be a nanny, Ronan."

In fact, she thought she might like to become more involved in Isabel's foundation. With Keely out of town, she'd started dropping in and was fascinated by the work the foundation did with various shelters, hospices and underfunded schools and she was touched by the impact Isabel's money made.

But moving in with Ronan was not a good idea; she knew this. Before the Wilsons, she'd stood on the outside of a family circle, looking in and longing to be a part of their world. Then, with her family in Auckland, she'd felt part of that inner circle and she'd loved it. But life moved the goalposts and showed her there was no place for her long-term.

Having what she most wanted, a family, and then losing it, had carved a chunk out of her soul. She wouldn't do that to herself again. It hurt too damn much.

"It's not a long-term solution, Joa, not for me, or for you. But it will serve both our needs in the short term.

It'll give you a place to stay that's not an impersonal hotel and something to occupy your time while you decide on the new direction you want to take. And it will give me time to find a decent, long-term nanny."

He made the whole notion sound so damn reasonable. And it would be, if they hadn't nearly set his couch on fire last night. "We made love last night…"

"So?"

Joa widened her eyes and her hands in a you've-got-to-be-kidding-me gesture.

Ronan looked down at his feet before lifting his head to look at her. "I admit, that took me by surprise. But, if you agree to work for me, for us, it won't happen again.

"Look, last night was an aberration. It had been a while and I got a little carried away but I won't let it happen again," he added.

He looked so damn sincere, sounded so determined. He really believed what he was saying. Well, hell.

"It shouldn't have happened last night. My boys were upstairs and had I been thinking straight, I would not have let it go so far, so quickly."

He looked like he was expecting a response but Joa had no idea what to say. She was both relieved and disappointed, annoyed and thankful for his matter-of-fact approach to their out-of-control, wildfire encounter.

"Uh-huh."

"So, is that a yes, a no? A go-straight-to-hell?"

Joa quickly tallied up the pros and cons in her

head. She didn't want to be alone; she didn't want to go to a hotel or to a furnished apartment. She really enjoyed Aron and Sam and it wasn't like she was committing herself to a long-term contract. She had to temporarily leave Mounton House, he needed time to find his forever nanny.

All pros.

On the con side, she still wanted to sleep with him. Like, desperately. He, on the other hand, seemed completely unfazed by their explosive sexual encounter.

And that pissed her off. Joa knew she needed to be sensible, that Ronan could mess with her head, mess with her plans. She was so attracted to him, a hundred times more so than she had been to any of her previous bosses. Looking back, and comparing what she felt for Ronan to those tepid feelings for Liam and Johan so long ago, she realized that she hadn't been physically attracted to any of those men.

Sure, it hurt when she left their employ and she mourned the dream of being part of a family, but her feelings had little, if anything at all, to do with the individual men.

Ronan was different. She liked his boys, sure, but she wasn't thinking "family" with him.

She was just thinking about having him, in any way she could get him. Preferably naked. And that was bad, very, very bad indeed.

She had to be sensible, she had to protect herself and her battered and bruised heart. Gathering her courage to say no, when she desperately wanted to say yes, Joa shook her head. "I'm sorry, Ronan. I don't think it's a good idea."

"Why not? Because you think I'll hit on you?"

No, because she was terrified that he wouldn't.

Joa told herself, once again, that while she might be strong enough to resist Ronan Murphy, she couldn't resist the voice message, sent from Ronan's phone, from his oh-so-serious older son.

She might have issues with Sam's dad but she refused to allow the little boy to think she didn't like him.

Stepping up to Ronan's front door, Joa rang the doorbell, stamping her feet and blowing air into her hands as she cursed the icy, snow-tinged wind. Would winter ever end?

Joa heard footsteps and told her excited heart, and ovaries, to calm the hell down. She'd seen Ronan the day before yesterday; there was no need to act like a teenager at a K-pop concert.

The door whipped open and Joa caught her breath, her words deserting her as she drank Ronan in. He was dressed in jeans and an untucked button-down shirt, and stubble covered his jaw. He still looked tired and harassed and so damn sexy.

"Joa. What are you doing here?"

Joa started to reply but a shiver racked her from head to foot and then she felt Ronan tugging her inside his warm house. "Man, you're an ice block. How long were you standing out there?"

Joa shook her head. "Not long. Stupid weather. I hate the cold."

"I can tell," Ronan replied, unwinding her scarf so that he could see her face. He smiled and pushed her knitted cap off her forehead. "There you are."

"Hi," Joa said, suddenly tongue-tied. Where had all her words gone?"

"Hi back," Ronan said, stepping away from her. "So, this is a surprise. I didn't expect to see you again."

"I didn't expect to be here but then I got a voice message from your phone." Joa pushed her hand into her coat pocket to pull out her phone and waved it at him.

Confusion passed over Ronan's face. "I didn't send you a voice message."

"I know." Joa pushed buttons and held up the phone. Sam's serious voice filled the space between them.

"Joa, this is Samuel McKenzie Murphy. My dad said that you can't be our nanny but he couldn't tell us why. We like you and we thought you liked us. So, anyway, me and Aron were just wondering what we did wrong."

Ronan tipped his head back and stared at the ceiling. When he dropped his head again, Joa shrugged. "I couldn't let them think that I didn't like them. I do, very much…"

Joa took a deep breath and, before she could change her mind, released the words in a heated rush.

"If you haven't made another plan for them, I'll do it. I'll look after them."

Ronan's mouth dropped open. "You will?"

"Yeah."

"Why?"

God, she didn't know. Because she liked being around people and living alone sucked? Because she missed her sister and she didn't know anyone else in Boston and she'd had the most fun with Ronan's kids? Because, while she could help out at the foundation, she wasn't employed there and there was only so much she could do?

Because she really, really wanted to spend time with Ronan Murphy?

"Am I too late? Did you find someone else?"

"No. Not yet…" Ronan rubbed his jaw, his expression still bemused. "I can't believe you are here."

Yeah, she couldn't, either. Ronan took a step toward her and lifted his hand to cup her cheek. His thumb skimmed her cheekbone and Joa sucked in a big gulp of air, leaning into his touch. This was temporary, she reminded herself, she would not dream for more.

Besides, Ronan was still in love with his wife. Great sex was just great sex, it didn't translate into there being a space for Joa in his heart. There never would be.

Joa took a step back and Ronan's hand fell to his side. Best to start as she meant to go on. Joa fiddled with her earring. "I'll also look for a long-term nanny for you."

"You will?"

Joa nodded. She'd thought about this. "Part of your problem is that it's *you* who is looking and *you* are doing the interview."

Ronan looked puzzled, so Joa explained that his famous name was, in this instance, a stumbling block. "If I take on the task, I will say that I am looking for a nanny for a client who has two small children, and you will remain anonymous until we find a couple of solid, genuine candidates. That will weed out all the ones who won't suit you or the boys."

"That might work."

Of course it would work. "And until I find you your paragon of nannyhood, I will look after the boys for you."

"You will?"

"Sure, they'll keep me busy while I look for my life's purpose."

"It's gone missing?" Ronan drolly asked and she saw a hint of the man Keely once called the greatest tease in America.

"Temporarily, I hope," Joa replied. She sucked in air and rolled her shoulders to release the tension gathered there. "So let's forget what happened between us—" hah! As if she could! "—and start fresh." She held out her hand. "Friends?"

Ronan arched his brows and looked down at her outstretched hand. Eventually, a million years later, he gripped her hand in his and pumped it once, hard.

"Yeah, something like that. Let's go find the boys. They are in the playroom."

What did he mean by that cryptic sentence? Joa followed him up the stairs, ignoring the photos of Thandi on the wall, looking so gracious and lovely and in love with her husband, her boys and her life. "I'll look after your boys, Thandi. I'll do my best, but only temporarily," she added, her words an indistinguishable murmur.

Ronan stopped abruptly to look back at her, and Joa put her hand on his back to stop herself from crashing into him. Beneath his shirt, she could feel hard muscle, feel his heat. She dropped her hand and surreptitiously wiped her clammy hand on the seat of her pants. "Sorry, talking to myself."

Ronan flashed her a smile. "You do that often?"

Joa flashed what she hoped was a cheerful smile. "How else would I get expert advice?"

Ronan laughed. "Fair point."

"Nice dress," Keely commented, holding out a glass of champagne.

Joa gestured to Sam and Aron, playing on the carpet by her feet, and shook her head. "Can't, I'm working."

"It's a party, Ju. Ronan won't have a problem with you having a drink."

Joa took the glass and put it on the table next to her elbow. She looked around the room filled with Carrick's guests, people who obviously knew the Murphy family well.

Tanna, the youngest Murphy sibling, was back in Boston and, judging by the heated exchanges between her and Levi Brogan, very much in love. In fact, between Tanna and Levi and Carrick and Sadie's hot looks, Joa was very impressed that the walls and drapes were still fire free.

"I'm not sure why I was invited tonight. I'm just helping Ronan out with the boys, trying to find him a nanny. I'm not part of your social circle."

"Social circle? It's a party with some friends, Ju. You are my sister and you're also Isabel's heir. And a Murphy client. And I've been friends with the Murphy brothers since we were kids. And Beah, Finn's ex-wife, is my best friend."

Joa cocked her head to the side. "How is she? I haven't seen her for, man, ten years?"

"She's good. She still works for Murphy's, but out of their London offices. She's their head of client liaison."

Joa wrinkled her nose. "Which means what?"

"She's the link between Murphy International and the client, advising them on what art to buy, what art to sell, what they should pay or sell the art for. She's really good at it, too. Her clients include Russian oligarchs, Arab princes, Asian billionaires."

"And she still works with Finn?" Joa asked, intrigued.

Keely rocked her hand from side to side. "Not really. She reports to Ronan. If she needs some information from Finn on provenance or history, they communicate by email."

Joa wanted to ask what went wrong with their marriage, but it had nothing to do with her.

"That really is a great dress." And because Keely changed the subject, she presumed she didn't want to gossip about Beah or Finn, either.

Joa looked down at the pretty, sunshine-yellow floral lace dress. It was shorter than the dresses she normally wore, the fabric sweeping from spaghetti straps into a V-neckline and from there into a fitted bodice. The flirty miniskirt ended midthigh, with a scalloped hem.

"The person who chose it really has excellent taste," Keely said, her tone completely serious.

"The person who chose it could've made sure it was an inch or four longer," Joa grumbled.

Ronan had issued the invitation earlier this morning, asking her to accompany him and the boys to Carrick's house for a cocktail party to celebrate Tanna's return to Boston. Keely, because she had the afternoon off, had been dispatched to find Joa a suitable dress. The yellow dress was the only one of the three that fit her properly.

"Thanks for helping me out," Joa said, squeezing Keely's arm. "By the way, I'm sending through a requisition for funding from the foundation to you. Can you approve it as a matter of urgency?"

"For what?" Keely asked.

Joa explained that she'd spent the morning talking through the renovations needed on a halfway house in East Boston with the house's director, who needed financial help from Isabel's foundation. With Keely being tied up in Florida, Joa had stepped up and taken over some of the decision-making for the foundation.

They really needed to find a new CEO soon. And she needed to find Ronan a nanny. When she met those two goals, she'd turn her attention to finding her own purpose in life.

"Sure. Thanks for taking over some of the foundation work, Ju. Between trying to sort out the estate and my speech therapy practice, the foundation has taken a back seat."

Joa didn't mind; someone had to evaluate the requests for funding, to make sure they weren't being scammed. And surprisingly, she'd found herself enjoying the work. She looked down at the floor and saw Aron's yawn; the small boy was fighting sleep. Crouching on her stilettos, she scooped him up and placed him on her hip. Then she dropped to her haunches again, balancing on her spiky heels to look at Sam. "Are you tired, honey?"

Sam shook his head but his tired eyes gave him away.

Sam yawned and Joa stood up, Aron's face in her neck. Holding out her hand to Sam, she walked across the room to where Ronan was standing, talking to his brother Finn and Levi, Tanna's fiancé. Tanna and Levi had announced their engagement earlier, and the guests were also told that Sadie, Murphy International's art detective, was pregnant with Carrick's baby.

It had been quite a night.

The men stopped talking as she approached. Joa handed them each a smile before looking at Ronan. "The kids are exhausted. If it's okay with you, I'll take them home, uh, back to your place. Maybe you can get a lift or call a ride?"

Ronan placed his hand on Aron's back. "Let me take him."

Joa shook her head. "He's fast asleep, let him be. If you can help me get them strapped into their car seats, I'll get them settled in their own beds at home."

She had to stop using that word. Ronan's house was not her home.

"Let's take them upstairs." Ronan saw the skepticism on her face and smiled. "After Thandi died, we moved back here for a few months and they often stay with Carrick. We'll put them down in my old room and Sam will be asleep in ten minutes."

"Really, Ronan, I can take them home—"

Again? Had she not just had this conversation with herself?

Ronan placed his hand on her hand and turned her away from Finn and Levi. "We'll get them settled and later, we'll take them *home*, together."

His tone suggested that she not argue, so Joa sighed, then nodded. Ronan picked up Sam and led Joa into the hallway and up the fantastic hundred-year-old staircase. Joa passed huge paintings on the wall, taking a moment to slide her free hand across the satiny wooden banister.

"Your family seems nice," Joa said as they hit the landing of the first floor. Ronan turned right and looked over his shoulder to send her a smile.

"They are nice. And I'm really happy that my boys are going to have a cousin to play with."

"Apparently, you were right about something sparking between Carrick and Sadie."

"It was pretty difficult to miss since they've only had eyes for each other since the day they met. I knew for sure when he got all flustered when I teased him about her that night I returned from China."

The night they made love. The memories of that night were etched into her brain. Joa followed him into a room with two sets of bunk beds. The walls were lined with a bookcase filled with books for kids and teens. Another set of shelves held a bunch of boxes containing cars and toy soldiers and board games. The beds were covered in brightly colored linen. It was a perfect playroom for two little boys.

"Nice room," Joa commented.

Ronan looked around and smiled. "This was the room Carrick, Finn and I shared from the time we were little until way into our teens."

"You lived here?"

Ronan nodded. "All of my life until I got married. This was our family home."

Joa looked at Sam and saw that he was fighting sleep. "Just put both of them into the bottom bed, it'll be easier to haul them out when we leave," Ronan suggested.

Joa bent over and gently placed Aron on the bed, pushing him over to make room for Sam. Stepping back, she allowed Ronan the space to do the same, and when he straightened, he looked at her. Joa sucked in her breath, astonished at the desire in his eyes. It danced between them, hot and tempting, and

Joa felt that delicious, sexual heat sweep through, her skin buzzing and her stomach jumping.

Ronan flushed and, grabbing her hand, pulled her out of the room into the dim hallway, spinning her around so that her back rested against the wall next to the door. He placed his hand on the wall next to her head and when he leaned in close, she tasted his breath, whiskey and toothpaste. Warmth rolled through her system and fireworks erupted on her skin.

"Ronan?" Joa murmured his name because she liked the sound on her lips.

"Mmm?"

"Please tell me you are going to kiss me," Joa whispered, entranced by the desire in his green-gold-blue eyes.

"In a minute." Ronan's other hand landed on her hip, trailed around, down her butt and up and under her skirt. He gripped her thigh, his big hand under her butt cheek, his fingertips on the inside of her thigh.

"This dress is dangerous," he growled. "Do not bend over in it."

"And what would you do if I did?" Joa teased, loving his sexy growl.

"Something like this…"

Ronan's mouth covered hers and his tongue slid into her mouth, twisting around hers in a kiss that was as desperate as it was hungry. His fingers on her leg inched closer to her happy place and his other hand covered her breast, kneading her nipple into a hard point.

His kiss deepened, became more ferocious, more demanding, and Joa forgot where she was, forgot that there was a house full of Ronan's happy relatives below her. She was consumed by his kiss, hankering for more.

For everything…

"Ro? Where are you?" Tanna's voice drifted up the stairs and Ronan pulled back, with all the tension of a stretched rubber band.

He stared at Joa, his eyes intense in the shadows of the hallway.

"Ro? Carrick wants to make a speech. We're all waiting for you, brother."

Ronan's hands left her and he stepped back, rubbing his hands over his face. He hauled in a deep breath, keeping his eyes on Joa as he responded to his sister. "Yeah, Tan, I'll be there in a second. I'm just getting the boys settled. Give me five and I'll join the family downstairs."

His words hit Joa with all the force of a meteor strike. His family was downstairs, his family was sleeping in the room next to them. *His* friends, *his* people.

People she had no connection to…

His family.

Joa heard Sam's call for Ronan and she forced a smile onto her face. Pointing to the stairs, she gestured for him to go. "I'll see what Sam needs, you go on down. Your family—" her voice hitched on the word and she hoped Ronan didn't hear it "—is waiting for you."

Nine

Organizing a last-minute date had never been a problem for Ronan, and even though seven years had passed since he last invited a woman to dinner, for a drink, it was as easy as it had ever been.

Janie was a divorcée he'd met at the kids' school and they'd become friends, mostly because she was the least obvious and in-your-face of the mommy crew. She'd let him know she was interested in seeing him outside of school hours, and now that he had both a nanny and a new attitude toward sex and dating, he could explore his options.

Making love with Joa had released the cork holding all his sexual impulses at bay, and in the week since that happened, he'd had a lot of time to process their coupling and the ramifications of that life-changing encounter.

Sex, as his brothers had been telling him, was a natural and normal urge and Ronan finally accepted the idea that he could...well, indulge. In his desperation to honor his wife and his marriage, he'd sublimated all those urges, bundling sex and love and marriage together. Sleeping with Joa had made him realize something he'd long forgotten: sex wasn't love and didn't need to be.

Sex was sex and he could share the physical experience with a woman other than Thandi, understanding that love and marriage belonged to her. And always would.

She wasn't here; their marriage was, on a physical level, over. He would always think of her as his wife but sleeping with someone else wasn't cheating on her...

He was sure it wasn't.

Ronan looked at the cool blonde sitting opposite him, felt a surge of panic and quickly reminded himself there was nothing wrong with sharing a meal with a nice woman. He was entitled to have a social life.

He couldn't sleep with or date Joa; she was his employee, at least temporarily. So he was going with plan B...

Ronan watched Janie's mouth move and nodded, hoping he was giving the right response. Since sitting down in this small, intimate West Roxbury restaurant, she hadn't stopped talking and he'd lost track of her conversation ten minutes ago. God, for all he knew, he could've agreed to a holiday in Saint Bart's or to buy her a house.

He really should concentrate.

"I insisted that Pasco be given extra reading lessons so he didn't become bored."

Ronan looked down at his perfectly baked fish and hoped Janie would, and could, discuss something other than her kids. This was his first date in so long and he would prefer to discuss something other than child-rearing.

He wanted to flirt, to laugh, to see if there was a chance of ending the evening with a bang... Ronan pushed away the image of Joa's perfect breasts, those responsive nipples, the citrus tang to her skin. Two kisses and one couch-based coupling and he couldn't stop thinking about her...

"And Michael is an amazing natural athlete. I have enrolled him with a private tennis coach..."

Blah-blah, yada yada. Ronan took a bite of his fish, keeping his eyes on her pale blue eyes, wishing he was looking into a pair of mysterious silver eyes instead.

Joa again. Ronan mentally threw his hands up in the air and reluctantly accepted that not thinking about Joa was an impossibility...

Janie was pale while Joa was darker, her skin a rich light brown with peach undertones. Janie's hair was short, streaked with various shades of blonde. Joa's was a straight, luscious fall, as dark as a sable coat.

Ronan looked down at his fish, thinking it tasted like sawdust in his mouth. Janie was just picking at the salad she'd ordered as a main course, taking tiny bites between long, overenthusiastic sentences.

He didn't want to be here; this wasn't any fun. And, let's be honest here, he didn't want to sleep with Janie, he didn't want to sleep with women in general.

He just wanted to sleep with Joa again...

But Joa, now working for him as his nanny, was completely off-limits. So if he wanted sex, he'd have to give Janie some sort of hint that he was interested...

Problem was that he wasn't interested.

Janie dabbed her mouth with her linen napkin and carefully placed it to the side of her plate. She leaned back in her chair and looked at him for a minute, maybe longer.

"You're not having any fun." Janie verbalized his earlier thought, breaking the tense silence.

"Uh..." Ronan inwardly cursed and wondered how to edge his way out of this conversational minefield.

Attempting to change the subject, he gestured to her plate. "You've hardly eaten anything. Would you like to order something else?"

Janie shook her head. "And spend another hour trying to rack my brains to come up with something to talk about? No, thanks. I tried to connect with you over our boys, the school, parenting in general, but you didn't engage with me at all."

That was because he was on a date, and he didn't want to talk about his kids. He was a father twenty-four seven; he wanted a break.

And they hadn't connected because he'd spent most of their time together thinking about Ju...

Crap.

Ronan pushed his plate away and took a large sip of his wine.

"Would you like to go?" he quietly asked her.

"No, but I know you do," Janie said, her voice soft but pride flashing in her eyes. She pushed her chair back and stood up. "Why don't you settle the bill while I visit the ladies' room?"

Ronan followed her to her feet and watched her walk away. The maître d' immediately approached him, concern on his face. "Mr. Murphy, are you leaving? Has the food displeased you?"

Ronan placed his hand on the elderly man's shoulder. "No, John, not at all. The service and meal were impeccable, as always."

Ronan exchanged casual conversation with John until Janie returned. Ronan flashed John a smile. "I'll see you again, John."

Sympathy flashed in the older man's eyes. "Thank you for joining us tonight, Mr. Murphy, madam."

"Add a good tip to the bill, John," Ronan told him, knowing that the restaurant had his credit card details on file.

John nodded gravely, murmured a quiet thank-you, but Ronan caught the flash of mischief in his eyes and sighed. He was about to make a decent contribution to John's bank account this month. Ronan placed his fingers on Janie's back to guide her to the door.

"Have a good evening, sir," John said, whipping in front of them to open the door.

He would. If he could get back to Joa.

Ronan tipped his face to the stars and shook his head. He had a dead wife, a failed date on his arm and he was thinking about his sons' nanny.

He was all kinds of messed up.

Joa heard the slam of the front door and the ping of Ronan's keys hitting the ceramic plate on the hall table. Sitting on the multicolored Persian carpet in the great room, she looked up as his big frame blocked out the light coming from the delicate French-inspired chandelier hanging in the double-volume hallway.

Being tall, he was a natural clotheshorse and she approved of his outfit of dark jeans, a checked brown-and-blue shirt worn under a flecked cream sweater, topped off by a well-worn but obviously expensive leather bomber jacket.

What she didn't approve of was the fact that he was dating.

Ronan Murphy was still in love with his wife and men who were still head over heels for their dead wives didn't date. Or shouldn't date.

Then again, neither should they have hot sex on the sofa.

Joa pushed a loose strand of hair behind her ear and looked up at him as he shrugged out of his jacket, throwing it onto the back of the nearest chair.

"You're home early," she commented, pulling her finger off the paper plate in her hand. She had glue everywhere, on her fingers, on her loose-fitting flannel pants, in her hair. "How was dinner?"

"Interminable," Ronan replied, resting his hand

on the back of the sofa opposite her. He looked at the mess on his floor—paints, glue, colored paper and markers scattered across the carpet—and frowned. "What are you doing?"

Ah, she'd been waiting for him to ask. "Do you recall hearing anything about the boys needing animal masks for Zoo Day?"

"What the hell is Zoo Day?"

"It's been in their communication book, on and off, for about a month now."

"Uh, I tend to forget to check that."

She'd realized that. "And because you didn't, I was reminded by them both, just after supper, that they needed masks. Aron demanded a chimpanzee mask and Sam, a tiger."

Ronan pulled a face. "I could just go and buy them one."

Joa shook her head. "That's not the way it works. It has to be homemade and the kids should've helped to make it."

Ronan sat down on the edge of the sofa and rested his forearms on his knees. "Dammit, sorry." He looked at the mess and picked up a paper plate she'd painted with orange, white and black stripes.

Ronan pointed to the mess surrounding her. "Do you need some help?"

Well, yes. Or she'd be here until dawn. Not giving Ronan time to rescind his offer, she handed him a piece of paper and a pair of scissors. It was the template for Aron's monkey mask. "Cut this out."

Ronan took the paper and scissors and without saying another word, began to cut. Joa glanced at the expensive watch on Ronan's strong wrist, surprised to see that it was only nine thirty. She wasn't going to ask why he was home so early; who he dated and what he did had nothing to do with her. They'd just had a one-night stand and it would never be repeated...

"That was a quick date."

Inquisitive much, Joa?

Ronan didn't lift his eyes off his task. "Yeah. We ended it earlier than expected."

"Oh."

Oh *was good,* oh *was noncommittal.* Oh *wasn't nosy. Good job, Joa.*

"Why did it end earlier than expected?"

Bad job, Joa.

Ronan's lovely eyes slammed into hers. "She was as boring as hell."

Joa winced, partly in sympathy for the unknown woman, partly because she wondered if he found Joa equally boring. After all, she was sitting in PJ pants and a tank top, bare feet, cross-legged on his carpet, making a kid's mask. Sophisticated she was not.

"She wouldn't stop talking about kids, hers and mine." Ronan rested the paper plate on his knee and pushed an agitated hand through his thick hair. He had lovely hair, nut-brown and glossy, with a wave to it that wouldn't be tamed. "I love the monsters, but I could've done with talking about something else, anything else."

"Art?" Joa teased him.

"Sure. Baseball, climate change, books, history..."

"Ancient or modern?"

"More modern than ancient, although I am partial to those bloodthirsty Vikings and randy Romans."

Joa smiled. "I've always been fascinated by the Russian Revolution."

Ronan resumed his task of cutting out the monkey face and Joa resisted the urge to rip it out of his hand and get it done. She didn't need perfection, just a rough outline. "Speed it up, Murphy, I don't want to be doing this all night."

"Bossy as well as beautiful," Ronan murmured. Joa felt her face heat and slowly raised her eyes to look at him, both frustrated and relieved when he kept his eyes on directing the scissors around the monkey's ear. Dammit, he shouldn't say things like that, sexy things.

Things that made her remember the feel of his hard muscles under her hands, the crisp hair on his chest, the rougher hair on his...

For crying in a rusty bucket, Jones! Get your mind out of the bedroom...

"What got you interested in the Russians and their revolution?"

"Don't all little girls want to be princesses?" Joa blithely replied.

"That family didn't come to a gracious end."

"Sure, but their lives, before the revolution, were amazing. To a kid who grew up hard, they lived a fairy tale. Well, up until they were shot."

Ronan cocked his head to the side, all his attention on her. "You grew up hard?"

Dammit, how had she let that slip? She never, ever,

not even with Keely, spoke about her past. What was the point of telling people that she was put into the foster system through sheer neglect, that she had no idea whether her druggie, far-too-young mother was alive or dead, that she'd been relying on herself for, well, all of her life? She loathed pity and she'd learned that sympathy didn't change a damn thing…

Her past was over, she was no longer a child and she didn't want to think about it anymore.

"I *grew* up," Joa replied, her voice tight.

"Where are your parents? Do you have siblings?" Ronan asked.

Joa tensed. "I grew up in the foster system," she reluctantly admitted, hoping he didn't press her for more information.

Ronan's expression held empathy but no pity. Thank God. "You don't like talking about your past, do you?"

"Do you?" Joa countered. "You lost your parents when you were young. Do you like talking about them?"

"I don't mind, actually. My parents were great, and it was a long time ago."

Good for him. Joa wanted to know more about them, but if she pried into his past, that would give him the excuse to pry into hers. Not happening.

Needing to change the subject, she returned to the subject of the Romanovs. "I'm not good at art and furniture but I have read quite a few books about Carl Fabergé." The imperial jeweler was an incredible goldsmith and produced some amazing works in gold and jewels. "He was so talented."

"That he was," Ronan agreed. "My father sold a Fabergé egg once."

"Really?"

Ronan looked at his monkey mask and handed it over. Joa handed it straight back. "Cut out the eyes, the mouth and the nose."

Ronan pulled a face and picked up the scissors again.

"What egg was it?" Joa asked.

"The Bay Tree egg. Nephrite leaves, white enamel flowers, diamonds, rubies, pearls. Lots and lots of diamonds. The surprise is a feathered bird that appears, flaps its wings and sings."

"Did you see it?" Joa asked, fascinated.

"It was before my time." Ronan looked regretful. "I saw photos of it."

"Wow. How does it feel to have had all these wonderful treasures pass through your hands?"

"Privileged, I guess, is the best word. Blessed."

Joa turned her head to the right and looked at the framed photograph of Thandi and her boys. "Do you see Sam and Aron going into the business, as well?"

"Carrick, Finn and I discussed this, just the other day, actually. We were talking about Carrick's baby and we agreed that if our kids want to join the business, if they are passionate about what we do, then we'll let them, agreeing that they would start at the bottom and work their way up. Kind of like we did. Well, not Carrick, but only because he was the oldest and someone had to jump right in when our parents died, but Finn and I had to prove our worth. But if our kids want to become lawyers or doctors or pilots, that's their choice."

Joa thought back to earlier when she'd caught Aron climbing up the double-door fridge to get into the snack cupboard. "I think Aron might become a stuntman."

"I think he might end up in jail," Ronan muttered. "He's his uncle all over again. Always chasing the next thrill, the next challenge."

"Carrick or Finn?"

"Finn." Ronan slid off the sofa to sit on the carpet, stretching his long legs and leaning back against the sofa. "Finn is going ice climbing!"

"Like waterfalls and stuff?"

"Yeah, that. Have you ever heard of anything that crazy?" Ronan demanded, looking completely irritated.

"Base jumping? Spelunking?"

Ronan reached over and tugged the strand of hair that had fallen out of her messy knot. "Don't be facetious. And he's done both."

Joa attached the last strand of wire to the plate—whiskers for the tiger—and looked at her creation. It would have to do. "Why are you so against Finn ice climbing?"

"It's dangerous."

"So is driving a car or flying an airplane or riding a motorbike," Joa pointed out, dipping her paintbrush into gray paint to color Aron's mask.

"Our friend Levi just broke his leg dirt bike riding," Ronan stated.

"Accidents happen." Joa shrugged. "And it is his life."

Ronan stared down at Sam's mask, his fingers tightening on the paper plate. "I can't lose anyone else. It would kill me, Ju."

"Is that why you don't date, why you refuse to look for love again?" Joa quietly asked.

"Yeah, it's a big part of it."

"What's the rest of it?" Joa asked, her hand shaky as she painted the mask.

"I'm still in love with my wife."

That wasn't news. Joa forced herself to look up into his eyes and was startled at the maelstrom of pain, confusion and irritation she saw in those deep green-blue depths.

Joa wanted to hug all his pain away. She felt herself leaning into him and then remembered she wasn't doing this again, she wasn't going to fall into his life and pretend it was hers.

It wasn't and it never could be.

"Learning to live again is hard, Ju."

Joa couldn't resist. She turned, rested her forehead on his shoulder and placed her hand on his hard thigh. The muscles under her palm flexed, tightened, but she didn't react.

What could she say? She was the very last person in the world qualified to give advice.

Ten

With ample warning that Joa had an important meeting at Isabel's foundation—a discussion with the board to look over the résumés for the new CEO of the organization—Ronan had asked Tanna, his sister, to collect the boys from school. It felt strange to have the afternoon off and to drive back to the house without the chattering boys in the car.

But the silence did give Joa time to think.

The candidates for the CEO position were, like the candidates for Ronan's nanny, just not right. Oh, they were all very qualified and very slick, but none of them possessed the amount of enthusiasm Joa felt was needed to run Isabel's beloved organization.

Like so many of the au pairs she'd interviewed, she felt they were all there for the paycheck.

For the boys, she wanted a nanny who would get down and dirty, who'd paint and play and talk to Sam and Aron, someone who'd interact on their level. For the CEO, she wanted someone who cared less about the glitzy benefits of the fund-raising parties and more about the people she, or he, would be ultimately helping. She wanted someone who would paint a room and serve food in a shelter, who'd stack books in a library, who'd visit the disaster-ravaged areas they funded. Good help, Joa was coming to realize, was very hard to find.

She whipped into the driveway to Ronan's house, noticing an unfamiliar car parked in her space. Pulling off to the side, she hurried up the steps, slipping her key into the lock and stepping into the warm hall. Calling out a hello, she dumped her coat and bag on the hall table, and walked into the hallway to see Tanna standing by the window of the great room. Ronan's half-sister was tiny compared to her big, burly brothers, and, like Joa, was a complicated mix of different cultures.

"Hey, Tanna. Sorry I'm late."

Tanna turned and smiled. "No worries. I took the afternoon off and I love spending time with the mini-monsters."

"Where are they?"

Tanna used her coffee cup to gesture to the garden outside, still covered with snow. Joa saw the boys crouched by a rock formation, fascinated by whatever an older woman was telling them.

Joa frowned. "Who is that?"

"Abigail Houseman," Tanna replied. "She said she had an interview with you about the nanny position?"

Joa thought for a minute and then winced. "Damn, I totally forgot about her."

She'd made the appointment weeks ago, when she first came to help Ronan out. Abigail, she now remembered, had been on a walking tour in Scotland and could only be interviewed when she returned. They'd agreed that if Joa found someone suitable, she'd email Abigail to cancel the appointment.

"What on earth are they doing?" Joa asked, confused by the boys' interest in a set of rocks.

Tanna laughed. "Abigail is giving them a history of gnomes in Boston. Apparently, gnomes live in boys' gardens and fairies in girls' gardens," Tanna said, with a completely straight face.

Well, that made sense.

Joa's lips twitched with amusement. "And the boys are buying it?"

"Aron is lapping it up, Sam suspects it's rubbish but he's enjoying the story." Tanna turned away from the window and headed toward the kitchen area, asking Joa if she wanted coffee.

Joa said yes and watched the boys for a few minutes more. Abigail looked to be in her midfifties, fit and slim. She wore her blond hair in a bob and was naturally attractive. Best of all, her attention was fully on the boys.

Aron had her hand in his and Sam's normally reticent expression wasn't anywhere to be seen. Joa instinctively knew they liked her.

Turning back to Tanna, Joa joined her in the kitchen and sat down on one of the stools at the island. "What do you think of her?" Joa asked.

Tanna thought for a minute.

"I really like her. She's easy to talk to, seems completely unfussy. The boys took to her immediately." Tanna pushed her cup toward Joa and her lips curved into a rueful smile. "I kind of interviewed her. I hope you don't mind."

She really didn't. The boys were Tanna's nephews and Joa appreciated a second opinion.

"She's fifty-nine, her husband died two or three years ago. No kids but she's taught grade school for thirty years and gave up work to nurse her husband who died of cancer." Tanna explained.

Joa felt a spurt of sympathy and asked Tanna to continue. "She's not looking for a live-in position as she has a house ten minutes away but she's not averse to spending the occasional night here if Ronan needs to travel for work."

"Did she say why she was looking for a job?"

"She simply loves kids and she's bored. She's traveled a bit since her husband died but, as she said, she's not the sitting-at-home-knitting or lunching-with-her-friends type. She doesn't want to go back into full-time teaching and she thought that a part-time job might suit her better."

Tanna's shoulders lifted and fell. "Honestly, Joa, I think she's perfect."

Oh, she sounded like she was. Of course, Joa

would grill her again before she recommended her to Ronan but Abigail did sound perfect.

Dammit, dammit, dammit.

Joa didn't want Abigail to be perfect; she didn't want to find Ronan his forever nanny because then Joa would be obsolete. She'd have to move on.

She'd lose her family.

No, dammit! Joa scrubbed her face with her hands, reminding herself that she was repeating past mistakes, that she didn't have a family, that this was a temporary position. She *had* to move on. She had to find her own spot of sunshine, her own place to stand. It wasn't here, in this house, with those boys and that man.

"So are you going to tell Ronan about her?" Tanna asked.

Joa pushed her coffee away and stood up. "I suppose I have to, don't I?"

Joa turned away and didn't see Tanna's satisfied smile.

Joa walked down the hallway of Murphy International, feeling out of place in her skinny jeans tucked into flat knee-high boots and a thick hooded sweatshirt worn under a quilted puffer jacket. The other women darting in and out of offices wore form-fitting dresses in bold colors, with neutral or skin-tone stilettos. But Joa had spent the morning at the halfway house, going over plans for the renovation, and she'd spent most of that time outside. Dresses and heels were pretty but impractical.

Office dresses and heels had never been her thing

anyway. She doubted they ever would be. She liked wearing flip-flops and sneakers, shorts and jeans. She couldn't imagine dressing up and slapping on makeup; she far preferred to get her hands dirty, whether it was looking after kids or climbing up ladders to inspect roofs.

Earlier, and still without telling Ronan about Abigail, she'd dropped off the boys at their school and headed to Isabel's foundation, joining the staff meeting already in progress. Thirty minutes in and they were still on the first item on the agenda. Joa made an executive, and easy, decision to move them along. By item number five she was chairing the meeting and afterward, the acting CEO told her that they'd achieved more in an hour than they had all week. They needed direction, Joa realized, someone to make decisions and to provide leadership.

She thought she just might be that person. She was passionate about the foundation, about the work they did, and she felt supremely comfortable in the role of CEO. But she wasn't qualified. She didn't have the business, accounting or management background, or any of the qualifications the board required.

But damn, it was fun. Running the foundation was something she could see herself doing for a long, long time...possibly for the rest of her life.

"Ju."

Joa jumped a foot high and slapped her hand on her heart. Catching her breath, she saw Ronan standing in the doorway to his office, arms folded across his chest, biceps bulging under his cream shirt, amusement dancing in his eyes.

"Holy crap. You scared me."

"You were a million miles away. What on earth were you thinking about?"

She might as well tell him and he'd confirm that she didn't have a hope in hell of getting the CEO position if she applied. Maybe he could help her find a way to still be involved with the foundation, to work with the new CEO, maybe as a consultant? She respected Ronan's sharp brain; she was sure he could help her figure it out.

"I was thinking about Isabel's foundation and how much I would like to run it," Joa admitted.

"What, as the new CEO?"

Joa nodded. "Crazy, isn't it? I'm not qualified, I don't have a business degree or know anything about accounting. And Keels is the one who can schmooze with donors—she can get blood from a rock. I'm not good at that. I feel out of place and tongue-tied at fundraisers, very much like the girl from the wrong side of the tracks."

She waited for Ronan to speak but when he didn't, she jammed her hands in the pockets of her jacket and tried not to let the disappointment show on her face. His nonanswer was an answer in itself. She wasn't suitable for the position. It was obvious...

"So why did you ask me to come down here?"

"We'll get to that in a minute," Ronan replied, his posture indolent but his eyes as sharp as razors.

"We're still discussing the open CEO position at the foundation."

"Well, I was. You weren't saying anything," Joa pointed out, a little peeved.

"I was thinking."

"And?" Joa demanded, wondering if she could slap a response out of him.

"I think you need to get over yourself," Ronan said, his tone and words blunt. "You're finding reasons why you can't take the position and you're missing the most obvious reason why you can."

"Sorry?"

"A, you can talk to anyone. You are one of the wealthiest women on the East Coast. People don't give a rat's ass where you or your money came from. The only person who seems to have an issue with that is you."

Wow. *Ouch*.

"B, so you don't have a business or accounting degree, but you have a brain behind that gorgeous face and great instincts. You can hire people to look over a contract, to dissect balance sheets, but finding someone who is as passionate as you would be impossible."

"But the board makes the decision…"

"Do you really think the board is going to vote against you and Keely, the two most powerful trustees? Tell your sister you want to do this and she'll persuade, possibly bully, everyone else to support you." Ronan skimmed his knuckle over her cheekbone. "Can I ask one favor, though?"

Joa blinked, trying to make sense of what he'd just

said. He hadn't dismissed her; in fact, he seemed to take her suitability for the job as a given. She had his unqualified support and, while she didn't need it, it was wonderful to have.

Empowering, heart-warming…

Joa remembered that he'd asked her for a favor. "Yeah, sorry, what do you need?"

"Before you join the foundation on a full-time basis, can you please, please find me a nanny?"

Oh, she had… She just hadn't had a moment to tell him about Abigail. And a part of her still didn't want to. She still wanted to be involved in the boys' lives, be able to pick them up from school, play Legos on the carpet, take them skating at Frog Pond.

She wanted to run the foundation, but she still wanted the boys. And Ronan, she wanted him most of all…

Joa's gaze met his and she watched as desire, hot and heavy, turned his eyes to a deep gold-green. Ronan's eyes dropped to her mouth and Joa shifted on her feet, her blood heating by a degree. He wanted her; she knew that. On the floor, up against the wall, anyway he could take her…

Oh, God, she wanted him, too. She wanted him in a big bed, rolling around, a tangle of hands and limbs and feet and tongues, creating sparks and mind-numbing pleasure.

Joa, feeling a little shaky, placed her hand against the wall because her knees had turned to mush and her brain to slush.

This man could send her from nanny to naughty in five seconds flat.

Not, on any planet, a good thing.

Joa swallowed, closed her eyes and counted to ten. Then she counted to twenty, telling herself she had to get it together. She was in his employ. She shouldn't be having naughty-but-nice thoughts about him.

But dammit, he looked like a sports model—six foot three of defined muscles topped by a masculine face. How could she *not* want to jump him?

Joa gripped the strap of her bag and held on for dear life. Dimly remembering where they were, she gave herself a mental slap and hauled in some air. She'd tell him about Abigail later. "So, was there a reason you called me down here?"

Ronan took a minute to make sense of her words and he eventually nodded, excitement replacing lust. "Oh, right! Yeah, there's something I want to show you."

Joa couldn't work out what he could possibly want to show her at his place of work. Their only connection, apart from their take-me-hard attraction, was the boys and the sale of Iz's collection. She wasn't an art buff and knew nothing about antiques.

"Okay." Joa shrugged.

Ronan threaded his fingers in hers, pulling her toward the bank of elevators at the end of the hall. He keyed in a code on the far right and when they stepped inside, Joa realized the elevator was smaller than normal and couldn't take more than two people, maybe three.

"Where are we going?"

"A secure storage room in the basement," Ronan

explained. "It's where we store our most valuable works."

She was still in the dark. "Why are we going there?"

Ronan ran his knuckle over her cheekbone, his abalone-shell eyes glinting with an emotion she couldn't quite read. Tenderness? Excitement? A mixture of both? "You'll see."

The elevator opened into a small vestibule and was guarded by a solid, opaque door. Ronan keyed in another code and the door opened. They walked into a massive storage room filled with shelves. In the center of the room was a long table and on it, packages in bubble wrap.

Joa glanced around, saw the cameras on each corner and raised her eyebrows at the security. "I feel like a hundred eyes are watching me."

"Not quite a hundred but, yes, this room is constantly monitored by our security team. Finn, Carrick and I are the only people allowed down here on our own and if someone needs to retrieve an item from storage they are accompanied by the head of our security. Everything that happens in this room is recorded from every angle."

Joa resisted the urge to wave at the nearest camera.

Ronan walked across the room to a panel on a monitor on the wall and Joa looked over his shoulder to see herself looking over his shoulder in the screen.

It was weird seeing what the security team was seeing...

Ronan pushed a button on the intercom next to the screen and when he spoke, his voice was strong and commanding. "Please cut the camera and audio feed to this room."

There wasn't a response but the screen was replaced with snow. Ronan walked over to the table and Joa followed him, dropping her bag onto a stool he pulled out from the table.

She looked back at the fuzzy screen. "You can cut the feed?"

Ronan nodded. "The art and auction world is highly sensitive and sometimes Carrick, Finn and I, or a combination of all three, have conversations down here that are highly confidential. We are the only ones who have the authority to order security to shut down the cameras and audio."

Joa sent him a small smile. "Are you going to tell me some sensitive company secrets? Please don't, I can't cope with the pressure."

Ronan grinned. "Nope, sorry. But I'm not sure if I'm going to be able to keep my hands off you and I'd prefer not to have witnesses while I kiss you stupid."

Joa's mouth fell open and it took her ten seconds, maybe twenty, for her to come up with a response. "Putting aside the fact that any sort of physical contact between us is not a good idea, and we agreed it wouldn't happen, you could've just taken me into your office and kissed me there. Why did you bring me to the bowels of the building?"

Ronan rested his forearms on the table and nodded to the cardboard boxes, openly amused. "Because of those?"

"I don't understand."

Ronan reached for a roughly shaped square and handed it to her. "Here, unwrap it."

Joa, still trying to understand Ronan's rather prosaic statement about kissing her, took the parcel and peeled the plastic away to reveal a photo frame.

Joa felt her breath hitch. The frame was square with bracket corners and a deep, vibrant royal blue. Each corner held a fleur-de-lis constructed from what could only be big, fat diamonds. In the middle was an oval cut out, framed in more diamonds.

It was obviously expensive, terrifyingly rare and undeniably breathtaking.

Ronan ran the tip of his finger along the edge of the frame. "So, as I'm sure you know, Carl Fabergé, along with his brother Agathon, took over their father's jewelry business. They couldn't manage all their commissions themselves, so they employed goldsmiths who managed their own workshops. Those goldsmiths produced a lot of items under Fabergé's name. This was made by a guy called Michael Perkhin."

"It's exquisite." Joa couldn't take her eyes off the frame, fascinated by the intricate detail.

Ronan gently removed the frame from her hand and gave her another parcel. "A world-renowned collector decided to thin out his collection of Fabergé and wants us to sell these items for him."

"Why would he want to sell something as beautiful as this?" she asked, holding up an earthenware container partly covered by silver scrolls and flowers. She found the silver lid and placed it on top of the bulbous container. "I don't even know what this is?"

"It's a ceramic tobacco humidor. It's special because it's by Fabergé himself and has the imperial seal."

Joa stepped away from the table and held up her hands. "I'm scared to touch it."

"Don't be. It's only worth more than three hundred thousand dollars."

Joa squealed and took another step back. "I'm not touching another thing!"

Ronan smiled and quickly unwrapped another parcel, sliding the tiny object into his hand before she could see what it was. Ronan clenched his fist and told her to hold out her palm. When she did, Ronan dropped the small object into her hand and Joa gasped at the miniature egg, festooned with diamonds and rubies, and edged with gold. It was designed to be worn as a pendant.

"Circa early 1900, marked as Fabergé, but accredited to one of his more experienced goldsmiths."

Joa examined the egg, running the tip of her finger on the bands of diamonds. "This takes my breath away."

Ronan took the pendant from her and placed it back in its box. "There's been a rumor circulating that one of the imperial eggs might be coming up for sale. We think that's why this collector is moving these items on, and if it does come up, he wants to liquidate some cash to bid on that egg."

"What would an egg be worth?" Joa asked.

"However much a collector would be prepared to pay for it," Ronan replied. "Ten, fifteen, thirty million? More? We won't know until it comes up for sale."

Joa spent the next twenty minutes inspecting each of the twenty lots, completely intrigued by the artistry of the objects. She took the loupe Ronan handed her and examined the diamonds, the emeralds, the fine detailing in the enamel. Then she went back and looked at some of the items again.

"I used to read about the Romanovs and the royal court, and about Rasputin and Fabergé. This world, for most of my fourteenth year, was my escape. I spent many hours imagining that I was an aristocratic Russian with a powerful father and a loving mother, cossetted and protected." She sent Ronan a quick smile. "I didn't have a great childhood. I spent most of my life in the system. Then I was a teen runaway."

Joa felt Ronan's hand on her back, but she couldn't look at him. She didn't want to see the pity in his eyes. "I find it so strange that I landed with Isabel, who surrounded herself with all the trappings of a wealthy, artsy world. That I'm standing here, looking at these objects, some of which I could, maybe, afford to buy."

Ronan walked around the table and placed his back to the table to face her. "How did you end up in foster care?"

She'd opened the door. She couldn't slam it in his face. She wanted to keep her past private, but she also wanted to tell him, show him who she really was. "Young, addicted-to-meth mother, father unknown. She tried to keep me. I have some very vague memories of bouncing between her and the system."

"Your dad?"

She shrugged. "I don't know who he was. She probably didn't, either. But he had to be of Indian descent because my mom was a blue-eyed blonde."

Ronan picked up a strand of her hair and rubbed it between his fingers. "How did you end up with Isabel?"

Joa picked up the egg pendant again and rolled it around her hand, focusing on the massive ruby at the bottom of the egg. "A foster mother who worked nights, a foster father who was losing the battle to keep his hands off me. I used to put a chair under the doorknob. One day I came home from school and the chair was gone and the lock to my bedroom was broken. I knew I had to get out."

She saw the anger in his face and it warmed her that he could feel rage on behalf of her teenage self. "I ended up at the shelter Iz funded, and she found me there. Two days later I was living with her and Keely. For the longest time, I thought of myself as Princess Anastasia, someone who'd escaped death." She shrugged. "I had an active imagination."

Ronan linked her hand in his. "I think you are amazingly brave. And incredibly resilient."

Joa finally lifted her eyes to his, grateful not to see any pity. "Thank you for not uttering any platitudes," she murmured.

"Yeah, I hate pity, too."

Of all the people who'd understand, Ronan would do it best. He seemed to accept that her past was in the past, unable to be changed.

It simply was…

Joa placed the pendant on the table and stepped up to him, wrapping her arms around his hard waist. She rested her forehead on his chest. "There's no point in looking back, Ro. It's not a pretty picture, so that's why I don't."

Ronan gathered her close. "I get it, Ju. I do. But I am sorry you went through that."

Joa snuggled in, happy to be held. It wouldn't last and, in a few weeks, she'd move on. But right now, he was here, solid and stable.

Ronan dropped a kiss into her hair. "Did you ever look at the list of items from Isabel's collection that are going to auction?" he asked, his deep voice warm in her ear.

Joa shrugged as she pulled back. "Sort of." It had been a long list and she'd been busy. "Why?"

"Isabel did own a miniature Fabergé pendant egg."

Joa pulled back and frowned at him, not sure if he was pulling her leg. "You're kidding!"

"It's silver, covered with gray guilloche enamel. Studded with diamonds. Circa 1910. Do you want to see it?"

"Hell, yes!"

Eleven

Later that night, Ronan jogged up the stairs to his third-floor master suite, feeling a hundred and four instead of thirty-four. It had been a long day and, thanks to spending two hours in the vault going through Isabel's treasures with Joa, he'd had to work late to catch up with reports, market research and various publicity campaigns.

It was now past eleven, the boys had been in bed for hours and Joa had retired to her suite shortly after dinner. She'd been quiet for most of the evening, pushing food around her plate, a million miles away. He knew the day had taken an emotional toll on her. He understood how difficult it was to open up, to talk about the past.

She was trying to plot her future, was dealing with

her past and how best to protect Isabel's legacy. He remembered Isabel as being acerbic and imperious but he'd always feel grateful toward her for giving Joa a home, for allowing her to feel safe. Every time he considered Joa, young and alone on the mean streets of Boston, his heart sputtered and stuttered.

The thought of an adult man entering her room and sexually assaulting her made him want to punch a wall. At various times over the past few hours he'd thought about checking in on her but he knew, better than most, that sometimes the kindest thing you could do was give people the space to be alone, allow them to work through their own issues in their own way.

So he was surprised to see Joa standing in the doorway to her guest suite, obviously wanting to speak to him. It was obvious she'd been doing yoga, maybe in his gym downstairs or in the living room area of her suite, because she was dressed in matching white skin-tight pants and a crop top and her skin glowed from exercise.

His cock, polite as always, rose to the occasion.
Stand down, dude, she's had a hard day.

Right then, Ronan realized he didn't want her to leave, not now, not next week, not ever. She fitted in his life, in his boys' lives; she made it better, brighter…

He liked her and, given some time, he might even come to feel more for her. The thought no longer scared him as it once had.

Serious food for thought…

"Ronan?"

Joa calling his name jerked him back to the present, to the fact that he was standing in the hallway, looking like an idiot. He rubbed his jaw and took a deep breath. "Yeah, sorry, I zoned out. What's up?"

Joa leaned her shoulder into the door frame and crossed one bare foot over the other. Her feet were long and delicate and tipped with fire red nail polish.

Sexy feet...

"If I wanted to, could I withdraw Isabel's egg pendant from the sale?"

Ronan nodded. "Sure, with Keely's approval. Are you thinking about doing that?"

She'd held on to the silver pendant egg the whole time they were looking at the more expensive items in Isabel's collection, like the Modigliani, the Degas sketch, the Vermeer. She'd appreciated Isabel's treasures but it was obvious that she adored the egg pendant. It resonated with her as a concrete link between her past and her real-life fairy godmother.

"I'm not sure." Joa bit the corner of her lip. "I'd like to, but I also feel like I should allow the pendant to be sold. It'll raise a lot of money."

"Honey, it might raise twenty-five thousand dollars, maybe more. Say it raised fifty thousand, a hundred thousand. That's a drop in the ocean compared to the many, many millions that will be raised overall. You could make a donation for the equivalent amount, if you wanted to.

"I heard you're pretty wealthy now," he added, teasing her. He liked the fact that she didn't take her wealth for granted. Or flash her cash around.

Finally, a smile hit her lips and her eyes. "Yeah, okay. I'll talk to Keely about pulling it."

Oh, Keely would be fine with it but, on the very slim chance that Keely objected, Ronan would buy the egg himself to ensure that Joa took ownership of that pendant.

"Do that, let me know what she says. Then send me an official email, pulling the pendant from the sale," Ronan said, trying to sound professional. Really hard when she was dressed in next to nothing and all he wanted was to pull those clothes off her...

"Ro?"

"Yeah?" His voice sounded rough, laced with sex. He wondered if she noticed.

Joa's eyes were big, round and full of emotion. "This sounds really strange, but when we hugged this afternoon, it was really nice. Can you, I mean, will you..."

She was asking him to hug her? She had to be kidding. "No."

At his sharp retort, the hot blush of mortification hit her skin, turning her face red. She immediately dropped her eyes and took a hasty step back, her hand on the door, ready to slam it in his face.

Smooth, Murphy. Not.

Ronan moved quickly to catch the door, staring down at the top of her head. She turned away from him, shoulders back and her spine ramrod straight. Now she was pissed.

He needed to explain and quickly. "I can't hug you,

Ju. Because if I do, I'm going to strip you, taste every inch of you and then make you mine."

Joa turned slowly and he saw the rapid rise and fall of her chest, desire in her eyes. She lifted one shoulder, attempting to be casual. "Okay. I'll settle for that…"

Ronan shoved his hands into his hair, tugging at the roots, trying to keep his cool. He needed his hands on her, his mouth on hers but first he had to make sure…

"Are you telling me that you want me, too?"

Okay, maybe he needed a little reassurance, to know she wanted him as much, but nobody needed to know that fact but him.

Joa didn't answer and he felt his stomach sink to his toes, disappointment rolling over him. Then Joa crossed her arms at her chest and gripped the edges of her exercise top, pulling it up and over her head, revealing her oh-so-very-pretty breasts with their tight, dark buds to his appreciative gaze. He clenched his fists to keep from going to her, wanting to see what she'd do next.

She didn't disappoint. Pushing her thumbs beneath the fabric at her hips and pushing her pants down her thighs, kicking the fabric away. Standing in a tiny pair of silky white bikini panties, she hesitated a moment before pushing the scrap of fabric down her hips. Her fantastic eyes slammed into his.

"Does me being naked count as a yes?"

He tried to speak but his tongue, for the first time

ever, was unable to form the words. Okay, well, then, he'd get his point across in another way, too.

Ronan lifted his hand and his fingers skated across her collarbone, down her chest. Ignoring her pointed nipple, he cupped her breast, lifting and tasting that smooth skin. He felt her back arch, trying to urge him to suck her, but his lips just curved across her skin. No, he was in charge here. He'd give her what she wanted, eventually, but he wanted to draw her pleasure out, tease and tantalize.

And be teased and tantalized.

Ronan placed his flat palm on her chest and gently pushed her backward so the back of her knees hit the bed, and she sat down. Keeping his hand on her chest he gently pushed so she was lying back, looking up at him, flashes of lightning in her silver eyes.

Ronan clasped her wrists and placed them above her head and Joa arched her back and lifted her hips. He liked that she wasn't self-conscious around him—she didn't need to be—and that she approached lovemaking as a natural, sensual act, nothing to be ashamed of. She might be skittish about commitment and have little experience of family life but she was a woman who liked pleasure.

And he intended to pleasure the hell out of her.

Keeping his clothes on—if he stripped he wouldn't be able to resist slipping inside her—he placed a hand on the bed covers next to her shoulder and loomed over her, taking in her perfect breasts, her flat stomach, the gentle curve of her hips and legs. Then his free hand followed his eyes, exploring the femininity of her shoulder, her narrow rib cage, and spent some time exploring her belly button. He spent endless minutes teasing her nipples, rolling them between his thumb and fingers, plucking them into even harder points. He wanted to kiss her, to give his mouth what his hands were enjoying, but if he did, this would be over in a matter of minutes.

He was on a knife-edge, his cock hard and straining against the fabric of his pants.

"Please, Ro."

Joa's slim legs fell open and he looked down, sighing. She was very pretty down there. He trailed a finger between her lips, heat rolling through him as he realized how ready she was for him. Dipping into her, pushing inside with just one finger, told him she was a flick or a slide or a kiss away from coming. Or even a word.

And if he gave her this, then he could start the delicious game all over again, building her up. Of course, there was the possibility that he would go off his head with need but it was a chance he was willing to take.

Ronan withdrew his finger and painted the inside of her thigh with her juices. Joa moaned her dissatisfaction and lifted her hips, wanting more, wanting everything.

"Ronan, I'm so close. Don't stop touching me."

Ronan pushed himself up so his face was above hers, enjoying the flush on her cheeks, the rapid pulse beating in her throat.

He did *that*. He made her hot and made her thrum, made her look like a wild woman. He was in his midthirties but he'd never felt more like a man than he did when he loved this amazing woman.

"What do you need, Ju?"

Those eyes drilled into him. "You, dammit. Now."

Ronan fumbled with the button on his pants, with his zipper. He wouldn't enter her, definitely wouldn't let himself come; he wanted this to last all night, but he could torture them both, just a little more.

Still only using one hand, and with Joa's fumbling help, he pushed his pants down and Joa pulled his shirt up and over his head. Ronan rubbed his cock over her and Joa release a soft series of *ohhhh*s and *Ro*'s.

Her voice sounded like an ocean breeze and her scent was an orchard of apple trees.

And when he pushed into her, she felt like home.

He'd pull out, he would, in a minute—there were still things he wanted to do to her—but for now, he'd allow himself to sink, to fall.

Resting his elbows on either side of her head, he brushed his thumbs over her cheekbones, rested his forehead on hers. This—being here, with Joa—was both heaven and hell. Heaven because they fit together so well; hell because he'd thought this part of his life was over forever.

Not wanting his mind to send him down that path, he dropped his head to kiss Joa's sensual mouth, all thoughts of right and wrong, past and future dissolving.

There was only now, and the present was perfect.

Ronan pushed his hand under Joa's butt, lifted her

hips and slid in a little deeper. This was as close as he could get, as far as he could go.

Feeling that familiar buildup at the base of his spine, in his balls, he gritted his teeth, telling himself that if he wanted to tease her, *them*, some more, he needed to pull out, to pull back.

"I love this, Ronan. I love your body. I love what you do to me."

Her words were softly spoken but she lit the fuse allowing his self-control to detonate. With an animal-like roar, something he never recalled himself doing, ever, Ronan slammed into her, a voice telling him to be gentle, to take it easy. But he couldn't, he needed to brand her, to mark her as his. Then Ronan realized her nails were pushing into his butt and she was lifting her hips to meet him, seemingly as desperate for him as he was for her. Wanting to test his theory, he slowed down, but Joa was having none of it. She jerked her hips up, taking what she needed, pushing up and into him, harder and faster.

Amazed by her passion, blown away by her need, he allowed her to control the rhythm and when he felt her ripple, when her channel clenched him, he started to move, long, sure strokes that were designed to maximize pleasure, to wring every drop from them both.

From far away he heard her scream, felt her blow apart, but then he was consumed by his own big bang, his own cosmic collision.

Pleasure, hot, fast and overwhelming, consumed him, and as he fell into that black hole of deliciousness, he felt Joa's second orgasm setting his nerve endings alight.

His head ripped from his shoulders and his heart blew out of his chest.

It took a long time for Ronan to search for his missing body parts, longer still for him to patch himself back together again.

Joa shot up in bed, felt the cool air on her chest and looked down, shocked to notice she was naked. Lunging sideways, she whipped her phone off her bedside table and forced her eyes to focus on the screen.

It was nine twenty...

Crap, crap, crap.

Joa checked her alarm, saw that it had been turned off and silently cursed the very absent Ronan. She'd fallen asleep in his arms—somewhere around three thirty, after three bouts of lovemaking, twice in this enormous bed, the last in the shower—her head on his chest, her hand on his stomach, her knee nestled between his legs.

She'd felt warm and happy and safe and sated.

Well loved and well used, in the best way possible.

Joa slipped out of bed and stretched, placing her hands on the floor and arching her back. Sex, she decided, was as good as yoga for stretching her muscles, for flooding her system with endorphins.

Walking her hands out, she twisted her head to the side, elongating her neck. And on the floor, half under her bed, was Ronan's shirt. After a few more stretches, she picked it up and slipped it over her head, pushing her arms down and smiling when the cuffs fell over her hands. She rolled back the sleeves and sniffed the collar, the scent of him warming her from tip to toe.

She'd amble downstairs, make some coffee and then come back up for a shower. Then she needed to go to the foundation offices to peruse some paperwork, and later this afternoon, she'd collect the boys from school. Maybe she could take them ice-skating on Frog Pond.

Joa walked down the stairs, trying to ignore the family photographs on the wall. It felt, yeah, *weird*, to be walking around half-naked in Ronan's house. Shrugging off her unease, she hit the bottom of the stairs in the hallway and deliberately didn't glance at the massive portrait of Thandi hanging on the wall to her right.

If she looked, she'd lose these wonderful morning-after tingles. She'd loved being with Ronan and loving him, and she wanted to hold on to those magical sparks still dancing across her skin.

Heading straight for the coffee maker in the kitchen, Joa popped a pod into the machine and shoved a mug under the spout. She hit the button and turned to open the fridge. And there, at eye level, was that damn note from Thandi to Ronan that Joa had read a million times.

Joa looked at the feminine handwriting, feeling her heart constricting. There were other notes under that one and, despite knowing she shouldn't, Joa pulled them out from under the magnet keeping them attached to the fridge.

Welcome home, honey. You've been in my thoughts. (But mostly in my sexual fantasies.)

Ro, I'll love you forever.

Kick ass at the auction, babe. We'll celebrate your record-breaking sales with bed-breaking sex.

There were more, but Joa had read enough. Replacing the notes, she felt her stomach lurch. She slapped her hand to her mouth, dry heaving. She slid down the fridge and wrapped her arms around her stomach, tears running down her face.

She was such a fool. A colossal idiot.

She'd fallen in love with another unavailable man.

Resting her forehead on her knees, Joa cursed her tears, mortified and disappointed with herself. She'd returned home to Boston with a clear vision, a plan to get her life on track. She hadn't planned on taking on more au pair work, determined to stop feeding her need to be part of a family by inserting herself into someone else's life.

She remembered thinking that she had money and a place to live and that she could afford to take the time to write the pages in this next chapter of her life. She'd planned on taking some time to chart a path forward...

But what had she done? She'd repeated past mistakes by not only taking another au pair job but also falling in love with, and sleeping with, her boss.

And this time she wasn't projecting, imagining, constructing a reality that wasn't there. She was irrevocably, comprehensively, forever in love with Ronan. She also loved his gorgeous sons.

But it was the man who rocked her world, who spun her around, who flipped her inside out. She loved his body, enjoyed his wicked sense of humor, his sharp brain and his easygoing-until-he-wasn't-personality. She respected his devotion to his boys and his loyalty to his wife.

His *wife*…

Joa's groan pierced the early-morning stillness of the house as reality, hard and hot and vicious, hit her. Ronan was still married in his heart, and probably always would be. Joa was the classic other woman, providing something Thandi couldn't, but there was no doubt that Thandi held his heart. Ronan would never love Joa as he did Thandi.

The evidence to back up that statement was everywhere. Gorgeous Thandi, a dedicated mother, was said to have been his best friend. Ronan still called her his wife, not his late wife, and the massive portrait of her by the front door announced to anybody who stepped in this house that she was still mistress here.

Her presence was freakin' everywhere. Fact: there wasn't room for anyone else in Ronan's life or his heart.

Ignoring the tears rolling down her face, Joa pushed herself to her feet and, carrying a heart as heavy as lead, made her way back up the stairs to the guest bedroom. She'd been so overwhelmed by Ronan last night she hadn't thought about where they'd made love but now it didn't escape her attention that they'd made love in the guest bedroom, she being the *guest*. She'd never even seen his bedroom, had no idea what was behind that perpetually closed door.

Joa walked into the en suite bathroom to flip on the taps to the shower. When the water was as hot as she could stand, she stepped into the glass cubicle, pushing away the images of Ronan's head between her thighs, taking her up against the wet tiles while she writhed and screamed.

She'd never seen his bathroom or his bedroom because those were spaces he'd shared with Thandi, hallowed ground.

She got it, she did. She understood that he didn't want those memories tainted, but it still hurt, dammit. It made her feel second best, less than. Joa would never be able to step into Thandi's shoes…

She was a girl from the wrong side of the tracks. She'd never felt like she belonged anywhere and she certainly didn't belong in this house, Thandi's house. Even if Ronan offered the opportunity to try, Joa would never measure up.

Scrubbing the scent of Ronan off her skin, Joa pushed down her tears and forced herself to think.

She had to stop feeling sorry for herself and make a plan… She needed to look after herself because she was the only one who could.

She needed to extricate herself from this house, causing the minimum of disruption to both Ronan and the boys. And she already had the perfect excuse to do that—she'd found Ronan's forever nanny. She just needed to set up the introduction. Abigail was kind, generous and suitable, and her presence in the house meant that Joa could move on.

While she was being honest with herself, she should accept that running the foundation as the CEO was just another pipe dream. Like Ronan, it was something she wanted but couldn't have. She wasn't qualified. Maybe she'd go back to au pairing, maybe not, but she knew that she had to leave Boston. She couldn't stay in this city; it would be too hard.

Luckily, she had time and she had money. She could figure out what she wanted from life as easily in Morocco or Monte Carlo as she could here.

She would drop out of Ronan's and the boys' lives, and soon she'd be nothing more than a pleasant memory. If she gave Abigail's name to Ronan, he would hire her—there was no reason for him not to—and they'd soon forget about her.

Ronan, if he ever thought about her at all, would remember her as someone who eased him back into a healthy sex life, a bridge between his old life and his new.

What she wouldn't do was give him a hint of the pain that was threatening to consume her, or confess her desperate wish to be his lover, to help him raise his amazing boys.

To share his bed, his life.

Those were impossible dreams, and Joa was, if nothing else, a realist.

Twelve

Across town, Ronan sat behind his desk, trying to concentrate on Eli's conversation. But honestly, he was only hearing every fifth word and nothing Eli said made any sense.

"Are you even listening to me?" Eli demanded.

"Not really," Ronan admitted.

Because thoughts of Joa, and the spectacular night they'd shared, kept invading his brain. Images kept appearing on the big screen of his mind: Joa's wet hair streaming down her back as he kissed his way down her spine, the tiny dimple in her butt, the fact that his hands could almost span her waist. The noises she made when she was about to come, the tenderness in her eyes.

Ronan was glad he was sitting down, that his pants

were hidden by his desk. Damn, he needed a cold shower. And a brain transplant.

Joa was his temporary nanny, a friend's sister, barely more than an acquaintance. He shouldn't be this consumed by her, thinking about her so much. He had work to do, kids to raise, an assistant to listen to. He couldn't afford the time to indulge in fantasies and memories…

No matter how amazing a night it was. No matter that he wanted many more of those nights…

"Beah should be here any minute," Eli said, standing up.

Ronan's mouth curved up into a smile. He'd never really liked Carrick's ex-wife but he adored Finn's ex, Beah, and Ronan had been sad when they called their marriage over.

Ronan had no idea why they never worked out but suspected it had something to do with the fact that Finn was as chatty as a rock and didn't wear his heart on his sleeve, or anywhere else.

Ronan looked past Eli and stood up as the tall, willowy redhead walked into the room. With copper-colored eyes and pale skin, she wasn't traditionally beautiful but there was something incredibly attractive about her. With her warm personality and stunning smile, she pulled people in and men routinely fell at her feet. Most of her clients were a little in love with her, but Beah stayed professional and they kept sending business her way.

Ronan stood up, kissed Beah on each cheek and

gestured for her to sit. "I was surprised to hear you were in town."

Beah crossed her long, long legs that ended in two-inch stilettos. "I need to talk to F...someone about a wedding, not a conversation I really want to have."

Ronan frowned. "Yours?"

Beah snorted. "God, no."

Ronan updated Beah on the news, both business and family, and then they turned back to business.

"I thought that, while I was here, I'd get an update on the Mounton sale and brief you on which pieces are generating the most interest with my clients," Beah suggested.

"Excellent," Ronan replied. Talking to Beah about her clients and art would force him to concentrate on work, would push his mind off Joa and last night. He was dealing in valuable artworks and he had to concentrate because making a mistake could cost Murphy's tens of millions or more.

He and Beah were nearly done when their meeting was interrupted by a knock on his office door. Annoyed by the disruption, he was surprised to see Finn stepping into his space.

Especially since Finn always seemed to know when Beah was in the building and did his best to avoid her.

Electricity crackled between them and Ronan eventually broke the sexually charged silence by loudly clearing his throat. Both Beah and Finn jumped and Finn jammed his hands into the back pockets of his jeans.

"Beah."

"Finn," Beah replied, equally formal. "I hope you are well."

"Fine. You?"

Dear God. Ronan wanted to bang his forehead on the desk at their stubbornness. Just find a room and get it done, was what he wanted to tell them but couldn't.

He'd told his brothers to stay out of his sex life, and what was good for the goose and all that.

Ronan pushed to his feet. "What do you need, Finn?"

"Not me," Finn said, looking miserable. "It's Carrick. He's holed up in his office, not taking calls or meetings."

"Is he sick?" Ronan asked, immediately concerned.

Finn shook his head and ran his hand through his shaggy hair. "I told him something yesterday, something about Sadie, and he's, well, pissed. Not at me, I don't think, but at the situation. I think he ended things with her."

Aw, crap. Carrick and Sadie were perfect for each other, any fool could see it. And if Carrick couldn't, then Ronan was the one to set him straight.

Ronan walked toward his younger brother and as he passed him, briefly placed a hand on Finn's shoulder. "I'll talk to him and see what's up. Hopefully, I'll be able to sort him out."

Though, like him, Carrick was stubborn. It might not be so easy.

Being stubborn was something all three Murphy brothers excelled at.

* * *

Ronan rapped on the closed door to Carrick's office but didn't bother to wait for an invitation to enter. Carrick, his forearms on his thighs, looked like shit. Judging by his bloodshot eyes and pale face, it was obvious he had a hangover from hell. But underneath, Ronan saw heartbreak, an emotion that had been his own faithful companion these past few years.

Carrick sat up and glared at him. "What's up?" he asked his brother, his tone curt.

"Marsha's canceled your meetings and is holding your calls. She's worried because the last time you cut yourself off so completely, Tanna had her accident."

Carrick frowned at him. "And you didn't think that maybe I needed some time alone!"

His brothers hadn't left him alone when Thandi died, no matter how much he begged them. In hindsight they'd been right—he'd needed them to be his buoy in a very wild sea. Well, it was time to repay Carrick. He'd never be able to fully reimburse him for all the long nights his older brother spent with him after Thandi died, but he could try.

"Want to tell me what's the problem?"

"No."

Ronan winced at Carrick's one-word answer.

"I want to be alone," Carrick stated, looking pointedly at the door.

"But what you want and what you need are two totally separate things." As he knew.

"I know what I need, Ronan."

"No, Carrick, you *think* you know. You think you want to be alone, to protect yourself from hurt, from having another woman leaving you. I hate to tell you this, but you can't control anyone's actions. People leave, people die and people mess up."

Jesus, where did that come from? And was he talking about Carrick, or himself? No, he had to be talking about Carrick because if he wasn't...

No, he wasn't ready to go there. He wasn't ready to let Thandi go.

She left you three years ago... She died, remember?

Shut up, inner voice.

Carrick tipped his head to the side and rolled his finger, gesturing for Ronan to keep speaking. Which, come to think about it, was strange. Like them all, Carrick didn't open up easily, and while they all argued about business all the time, they didn't talk much about their personal lives.

"You and Sadie called it, didn't you? Or, to be more precise, you did." He wanted to tell Carrick that he was a complete moron for letting Sadie slip away but he knew that Carrick would either kick him out or punch him and Carrick would stew in his stubbornness.

Carrick needed Sadie, dammit. He deserved a second chance at marriage, to be happy.

Didn't they all?

Carrick shrugged and Ronan felt a surge of frustration. "She was your one, Carrick, the person meant for you. How can you not see that?"

"How do you know?"

Was Carrick really going to make him explain? Well, if talking sliced through his brother's stubbornness, he'd give it a shot. "Because I know true love when I see it, Carrick! I lived it, I had it and I recognize it. She is your other half, the person you are supposed to be with."

"I thought the same with Tamlyn."

Ronan didn't know how Carrick could compare the bright, funny, lovely Sadie with his ex-witch. Annoyed, the words tumbled out of him. "You don't only get one person to love and you love people differently, at different times of your life. You loved Tamlyn, but you're a different person now to the person who loved her. You don't only get one shot at marriage and love, Carrick."

Ronan heard his words, knowing he was walking straight into a trap, a trap his brother wasn't going to let him wiggle out of. "I hear you, Ronan, I do."

Okay, maybe Carrick was too deep in his own misery to toss Ronan's words back in his face.

"So, you are going to sort out this mess with Sadie?"

"I am. But before I do, can I ask you one question?"

Ronan nodded, then shrugged. "Sure."

"Why is there one set of rules for me and a different set for you? If I get to take another shot at a relationship, why can't you?"

* * *

"Why is there one set of rules for me and a different set for you? If I get to take another shot at a relationship, why can't you?"

After leaving Carrick's office, the tough question burning in his brain, Ronan walked straight to his car and headed home, needing to be where Thandi was. Because Thandi wasn't in a grave; she lived within his sons, in the memories they shared in their West Roxbury house, in the rooms she'd walked and lived and loved in.

Before entering, he'd checked his security cameras and knew that Joa wasn't home. She'd left somewhere around eleven and, hopefully, she wouldn't be back anytime soon. He needed time alone, time to think.

With Carrick's question floating around in his brain demanding an answer, Ronan entered his house, thinking that he was seldom here when the kids weren't. Ronan didn't bother to shed his coat; he just stood in front of Thandi's portrait, the first thing anyone saw as they walked into his house. His beautiful wife, the beat of his heart.

Was she, still? Was he still in love with her? Oh, he still loved her but was he still *in love* with Thandi?

If I get to take another shot at a relationship, why can't you?

He'd gone into Carrick's office to straighten him out but he'd been the one who'd come out of that encounter feeling scathed and shot, his entire world upended. He'd been so damn arrogant, telling Carrick he had a right to another relationship, that he was throwing away the chance of happiness because he'd had a bad marriage with a bad woman.

You don't only get one person to love and you love people differently, at different times of your life.

Did that mean he was allowed to fall in love again? Could he? Was Joa the one he could take that chance on?

Ronan turned his gaze onto the photograph on the hallway table, the photograph of he and Thandi on their wedding day. They'd been so happy. Could he even be half as happy with someone else?

Yet he had been, these past weeks, with Joa. A different type of happy. Not better or stronger, just different. Ronan looked into the great room, saw the many photographs of Thandi on the mantelpiece, the massive silver frame on top of the piano. There were photos of her on the fridge. In fact, there were photos of her everywhere.

Ronan mentally moved up the stairs, picturing the photos of her on the walls, photos of her on the table on the landing, photos of her scattered around his bedroom. What did people think when entering his house? How did they feel about being surrounded by images of his dead wife? His entire house was a shrine to Thandi, and maybe it was time to let her go.

Time to embrace something, *someone* different.

Maybe it really was time for him to start living again…

Ronan turned at the sound of the front door opening and his heart rate accelerated as Joa stepped into the hallway, black hair glinting in the sunlight streaming in from the glass insert above the door. She looked surprised to see him, then her face settled into a bland expression, the expression she used to put distance between them.

Joa was acting like his employee, like his reticent nanny. He wanted the warm, exciting, hot-blooded woman who'd shared his bed last night, not this cool beauty with flat eyes and a taut mouth.

"What are you doing home?" Joa asked, placing her bag on the hall table. She never hung anything up. It should annoy him, but it didn't. He was just happy she was there, sharing and messing up his space.

How could he explain? How would she react if he told her that she brightened his life, that he wanted to see whether they could, maybe, make this work? That he thought he might be falling in love with her...

"Uh..."

Joa jammed her hands into the pockets of her coat and rocked on her heels. She stared at a spot past his shoulder and later, when he remembered this conversation, he'd pinpoint this moment as the start of their downward slide. Before he could form any words, she spoke. "I think I've found you a nanny."

Ronan felt like she'd punched him in the gut. He'd totally forgotten her search for a nanny. "I thought you liked my kids, that you enjoyed looking after them."

"Ronan, I told you this was temporary. That I didn't want to be an au pair anymore."

Well, yeah, she had said that...

"She's really rather wonderful. She's a grade

school teacher, and the boys really like her. She lives close by…"

He didn't want another nanny, he wanted *her*. "I don't care. I want you to stay."

Ronan knew, from a place far away, that he was botching this, that he needed to explain, but his feelings were too new, too fragile. He hadn't had any time to work through his thoughts, to come to terms with the idea that he could be happy again, with someone else, that he could put aside his guilt and start to live again. He needed to do that, he needed time, but he also didn't want to lose Joa. Because, God, if she left him, left this house, she might get on a plane to Bora-Bora or Brisbane, Taiwan or Tennessee. If she left, he wouldn't be able to get her back.

"Best thing is, she can start straight away," Joa said, ignoring his previous comment. "I've arranged for her to pop around tonight. You can meet her then."

"I don't want her, I want you!" Ronan roared.

His bellow didn't scare Joa; she just planted her feet and kept her gaze on the wall behind him.

"Will you damn well look at me?" he shouted. He gestured to Thandi's portrait. "I'm here, she's not!"

Joa finally wrenched her eyes off Thandi's portrait. "Of course she is, Ronan. She's everywhere. In your head, in your house, in everything you do, every decision you make."

Joa held up her hand and tossed her head, blinking back tears. "It's okay, Ronan. It really is. I get it. She was the love of your life, the mother of your kids. I can't compete with that. I don't want to compete with her."

Ronan wanted to tell her that he loved them differently—he *loved* Joa? Jesus, did he? Maybe…

Man, this was all too much, too soon. He felt like he was being emotionally sideswiped from all angles.

"Let's not make this more difficult and emotional than it needs to be, Ro. Let's keep this simple, okay?"

Simple sounded good. It really did. Simple was him living his life as a widower, alone. Raising his boys, working, his life uncomplicated by a silver-eyed goddess who made his blood sing. He liked simple. Simple made sense.

But simple was also boring, unimaginative, lonely…

"I know that Tanna is taking the boys to spend the weekend at the Lockwood estate. They've been invited to Darby's stepdaughter's birthday party."

Ronan rubbed his forehead with the tips of his fingers, trying to think. Yeah, that sounded right. God, he was so tired. He felt like he could sleep for a week…

He'd forgotten how exhausting emotions could be.

Joa pushed her hands into the pockets of her coat. "I've booked a flight to go to Miami, to spend the weekend with Keely. There's so much we need to discuss with regard to the foundation, including a very impressive résumé we received today. The applicant might be perfect for the CEO job."

No, that job was Joa's. Nobody was better suited to running Isabel's foundation than the resilient, amazing girl-turned-woman whom Isabel had rescued all those years ago. Ronan wanted to tell her that, insist that she fight for the job, but he couldn't form the words because there were so many others on his tongue.

Don't go.

Don't leave.

I think I'm falling in love with you...

Joa sucked in a breath, emotions he couldn't identify tumbling through her eyes and across her face. "Interview Abigail tonight and if you like her, why don't we all go out to dinner on Sunday night? You, the kids, Abigail and me. We can tell them that Abigail will be their new nanny. And I can say goodbye."

The thought of her leaving them—*him*—forced his brain to kick into gear and form some words. "You're leaving? Where are you going?"

Joa shrugged. "I don't know yet. I'll see. But I think it's best if I leave Boston, put some distance between me and my memories of Iz."

Put some distance between you and me. Ronan heard the words as clearly as if she'd spoken them.

"Are you really leaving me?" Ronan asked, feeling like she'd reached into his heart and yanked it out of his chest.

Joa swallowed, closed her eyes and nodded. Her "yeah" was small but still audible.

"Did you hear me when I said that I want you?" Ronan asked, his voice cracking.

Joa placed her hand on his heart, a touch that briefly cut through the cold fog enveloping him. "I

know you want me, Ro. That was never the problem.
But what I want the most belongs to someone else and
I'm not going to fight her for it."

Joa turned away and Ronan watched her walk up
the stairs, feeling overwhelmed, a little pissed and totally at sea. He started to go after her, suddenly terrified by the thought of her not returning. What would
he do? How would he cope? Oh, this had nothing to
do with her looking after the boys, and everything to
do with where he wanted her in his life...

No!

Not yet, think it through.

Ronan knew he couldn't be impulsive. He couldn't
go on his gut. He had to think, pick this situation
apart. He couldn't throw himself at her feet, because
she was vulnerable, too, and might agree to stay, to
move into his life, his world, as his partner and lover,
not just as a nanny. And, when the novelty of fantastic sex faded, would one or both of them realize that
they'd made a huge mistake?

He couldn't just think about himself. He had the
boys to consider.

He needed to think, dammit. Ronan scrubbed his
hands over his face and was surprised to feel the
hint of tears on his cheeks. Tears? Really? He had
never thought he'd cry again, and especially not over
a woman.

Ronan dropped his hands and his gaze landed on
the silver photo frame, the picture of him, Thandi and
Sam, back when he was completely happy, so damn
sure of himself and his place in the world.

Ronan placed his fingertip on Thandi's cheek, ran it over her jawline and then slowly and deliberately lay the photograph facedown.

Thandi was dead, and life, so it was said, was for the living.

So that begged the question, how was he going to live his?

Thirteen

Joa stared past Keely's shoulder to the placid Atlantic Ocean behind her.

It was Saturday afternoon or, as Joa liked to call it, day two of her crappy, Ronan-free life.

She'd have maybe an hour or two more with Ronan and the boys when they had dinner tomorrow night and then she'd leave their lives forever.

Forever.

God, that was a long, long time.

She didn't know if she could bear it. She'd been so stupid, falling in love with a man who was unavailable. When was she ever going to learn?

Keely looked up from reading the résumé of the latest applicant for the foundation's CEO position and rolled her eyes. "Are you going to spend the entire weekend sighing?"

"Probably," Joa admitted, lifting her glass of iced tea to her lips. She gestured to the résumé lying across Keely's thighs. "She sounds great, doesn't she?"

Keely tapped the paper with her index finger and shrugged. "You seem to think so."

"She's smart, has the right qualifications and has a solid track record of working in the sector," Joa countered. "She's perfect for the job."

"Or you *want* her to be perfect for the job," Keely said, tossing the résumé onto the wooden table between them. They were seated on the deck of Keely's luxurious rented house and it was so nice to be in shorts and flip flops again.

Well, her body was warm; her heart still felt like it was encased in ice. *Might as well get used to the sensation, Jones.*

"What are you trying to say, Keely?"

"Her being so great gives you the out you're looking for."

Joa tried to make sense of her words but came up blank. "I'm sorry?"

"You want her to be wonderful so you can leave Boston, the foundation, me," Keely stated, her voice holding an edge that Joa had seldom heard before.

"You left out Ronan and his boys and Mounton House and Boston and Isabel's memory," Joa quipped. When Keely's eyes turned stormy, Joa realized Keely didn't appreciate her flippancy. But Joa had to pretend everything was fine, because if she didn't, she'd curl up in a ball and sob.

"Oh, we'll get to Ronan in a minute," Keely crisply told her. She leaned forward and nailed Joa with a sit-there-and-listen stare. "When are you going to stop running, Joa?"

Wow. That was unfair. "I am not running. And how did we get onto this subject? We were talking about the CEO position."

"A position that you want, that you would be so good at!" Keely's voice rose.

"I'm not qualified, Keely."

Keely threw up her hands in frustration. "Oh, sure, you couldn't possibly acquire some new skills. You don't have a brain in your head, and you *only* have a master's degree in psychology. Yeah, you couldn't *possibly* learn anything new. And we couldn't possibly afford to pay for any advice we might need."

Wow, while she was gone Keely had become very proficient in sarcasm.

"Uh...you'd support me running the foundation?"

Keely overexaggerated her eye roll. "Argh! Yes! You have passion and empathy and you get what Isabel was trying to do. I kept an eye on the foundation while you were away because someone had to, but it's not what I want to do. You, however, just jumped in feetfirst."

She had. And it *was* her dream job, her connection to Iz, to her past. But if she chose to take the job, and it seemed like it was hers if she wanted it, she'd have to stay in Boston.

Staying in Boston would mean she would, occasionally, run into Ronan, as she explained to Keely. That meant being around someone, three someones, she couldn't have.

"And why can't you have a relationship with him and the boys?" Keely asked. "Any fool can see you two have a connection."

"He's still in love with his wife," Joa muttered.

Keely held up her index finger and pointed it at Joa. "Oh no, you can't blame all of this on him. You have your issues, too."

"Which are?"

"You're terrified to be all in with someone."

"Can you blame me since I was hurt every time I left a family?"

"It couldn't have hurt that much," Keely retorted, "or else you would've stopped au pairing a long time ago. But you didn't leave until you were asked to leave because you felt safe there. You could love your boss from afar, pretend you were part of his family, act out your happy-family fantasies because there was no chance of anything happening, no risk to you. Because a real family comes with the *potential* of heartache, with the potential of someone leaving you, someone not loving you. Pretending is so much easier, so much safer than actually living."

Joa stared at Keely, her mouth opening and closing, feeling hot, then cold. She wanted to argue, to tell Keely she was talking nonsense, but Joa couldn't. She'd never considered *why* she fell for unavailable men.

Her sister was right. Joa had been trying to protect

herself, to put a barrier between her and any potential loss.

Ronan had started to say something about wanting her to stay, but because she was scared, because that conversation felt too real, too scary, she'd tossed Thandi in his face and made his dead wife the barrier between them.

Maybe Ronan did still love Thandi, maybe he wasn't ready to move on with Joa or anyone else, but she didn't know for sure because she hadn't given him a chance to explain.

She had just run out of there because what she felt for him was so damn tangible. Tangible meant scary. And she hated feeling scared, vulnerable, like she was fourteen again, and alone.

Joa didn't realize that tears were running down her face until Keely touched them with her fingertips, wiping them away. "I'm not telling you that he loves you, Ju. I don't know if he does or doesn't. But he hasn't looked at anyone else in three years the way he looks at you. I haven't seen him this happy for the longest time. I haven't seen you glow like this for years and years. There's something there and you owe it to yourselves to explore it, to see where it goes."

Joa placed her elbows on her thighs and her hands on her head. "I hear you, Keely, I do. And I know that I run away to keep myself safe. But she's still such a big part of his life..."

"She's the mother of his kids, babe. She'll always have a special place in his heart." Keely pulled a face. "And maybe he'll never be able to love you the way you need him to, but you can't run without giving him the chance, or at the very least, without talking to him about the way you feel."

Joa's heart bounced off her chest. "Are you saying I should tell him that I love him?"

"If that's how you feel," Keely replied. "He might, or might not, love you back. But that's his choice. Your choice is to tell him how you feel. It's also your choice to take the job you love and not let him, or the way you feel about him, influence your career."

"Ooh, ouch. The punches keep coming."

Keely squeezed her knee. "The truth is an ugly thing, baby girl." Keely rested her forehead on Joa's knee before sending her a sympathetic smile. "You need to be brave, Ju. You need to take a chance on *something*. And you need to start living in the real world, not a pretend one."

The truth was undeniable, but it wasn't fun. Or fair. Or easy or nice. But it was the truth. And if she wanted to look at herself in the mirror with any sense of self-respect, she had to face it and deal with it.

A few months shy of her thirtieth birthday and she finally, emotionally, felt like an adult.

Ronan taped down the bubble wrap on Thandi's portrait and looked at the bare spot on the wall. He'd expected to feel sad, but really he just felt…content. Like it was time to let his wife go.

Thandi wasn't in a picture on the wall, she was in Sam's smile and Aron's eyes and in the million memories Ronan had of her.

He felt Carrick's hand on his shoulder and Finn

moved to stand on his other side, and he was grateful
for his brothers' presence. He'd unhooked pictures off
walls and taken them off sideboards and tables and
corkboards—leaving the silver frame containing the
picture of Thandi and Sam—Aron in her huge tummy
so he was there—on the table between his boys' beds.
Ronan had removed all the photos from his own bedroom and put Thandi's notes from the fridge in a shoe-
box, along with the other unframed photographs he
found along the way. The framed photographs were
packed into the cardboard boxes at his feet.

But he'd needed help to take Thandi's massive portrait off the wall and there were only two guys he
could ask to help him with that.

Carrick looked at the bare spot and grimaced.
"You definitely need a painting to cover that spot."

"Can't think where we might be able to source
one," Finn replied, his tongue in his cheek. The attic
at their family home, the house Carrick inherited and
lived in, was crammed with art.

Correction, the house Carrick and Sadie now lived
in. And Carrick was so besotted with his new fiancée that Ronan knew he could ask for anything and
Carrick would hand it over...

"I've always been partial to the landscape on your
bedroom wall." Ronan teased, knowing it was one of
Carrick's favorite paintings.

"Let me think about that..." Carrick held up his
index finger, "mmm...no."

Oh, well, it was worth a try.

Ronan shrugged. "I'll find something." He looked

at the empty space on the wall, hauled in a deep breath and folded his arms. "What do I tell the boys when they ask where their mom has gone?"

"If they even notice, you tell them the truth. That there's a photo of her in their bedroom if they need to look at her," Carrick replied. He nodded to the big boxes containing the rest of the frames and photographs. "Do you have space to store these boxes or do you want them to go into the vault or up into the attic at the house?"

Ronan was grateful that neither of his brothers suggested getting rid of the photographs. They understood that Sam or Aron might want them someday. Hell, he might want to look at them again, although he had copies of all of them in his cloud account.

"I'm not sure yet," Ronan replied, rubbing the back of his neck. "Can I let you know?"

"Sure." Carrick walked into the great room and headed straight for the cupboard in the kitchen where Ronan kept a bottle of Jack. After grabbing three tumblers, he poured them each a shot. Passing the glasses out, he raised his. "To Thandi. May she rest in peace."

Ronan nodded, touched. "Yeah."

Finn tossed his drink back and rested his forearms on the granite counter of the island. "Are you going to tell us what prompted this, Ro?"

Ronan pushed his hand through his hair. "A combination of things. I thought it was time to say goodbye, to let her go. Partly because of Joa..."

"How's that?" Carrick asked.

"Well, it can't be fun walking into your lover's house and seeing his dead wife on the wall. On *every* wall."

"Fair point." Finn agreed. "So, does that mean you are going to try and work it out with her?"

Ronan shrugged. He'd missed her terribly these past two days and couldn't wait to see her later. But he wasn't sure if he was rushing into things. Maybe he just thought he was in love with her because she was the one who'd broken through his icy walls. He explained his dilemma to his brothers, both of whom took a minute to give him their considered and thoughtful opinion.

"Bullshit."

"Horse crap."

Well, okay, then. Carrick poured another shot, but Ronan shook his head. It had been a hell of a day already and his boys would be arriving any minute from their weekend away with Tanna at the Lockwood estate. And later, they'd all be going out to eat. He most definitely needed his wits about him.

"You're looking at this wrong, Ro. Maybe she was the one who broke through because she was the only one who could. Despite being our resident charmer, you've never been a player. You've always taken love and relationships very seriously." Carrick held up his hand. "That's not a criticism, just a statement of fact. You take a while to fall in love but when you do, nothing much budges you off it."

"Yeah, Joa has to be special for you to do all this. To move on," Finn agreed. "If she wasn't, you wouldn't be doing this. And I think Thandi would approve. I think that, had she met Ju, they'd be friends."

They were completely different people, but he agreed. They would've been friends. Ronan pulled in a deep breath, trying to ignore the prickle of heat in his eyes, the slight burn. "Thanks. For being here... For doing this. For—" Jesus, his voice was cracking "—you know, everything."

"You should be grateful since I left my brand-new fiancée to be here." Carrick's fist smacked his arm. Ronan audibly cursed Carrick but silently thanked him. Had he not punched him they might all be in tears by now. They all preferred pain to pathos.

Finn snickered. "You should be grateful to Ronan for giving you a damn fine excuse to take a break from Sadie. You're not as young as you used to be, Carrick."

Carrick nailed Finn with a hard look. "Bastard."

Finn's phone beeped and he pulled it out. He swiped the screen, read the message and cursed. Happy for the change of subject, Ronan asked him what the problem was.

"Obviously you remember Ben? He spent a lot of time at our house when I was a teenager?"

Ronan nodded.

Finn continued. "Well, he and his girlfriend from way back then have recently reconnected. They both ended up working for the same company in Hong Kong and are getting married. But because they are there and not here, they want me to organize their wedding."

Ronan exchanged a glance with Carrick, thinking that there was more to the story. But he couldn't help laughing at Finn's uncomfortable expression. "Really? You?"

Finn looked miserable. "No, Not only me. Beah's going to help me since Ben and Piper attended our wedding ceremony in Vegas."

Carrick frowned. "About that…"

Finn rolled his eyes. "It happened nearly ten years ago and we got divorced. You can't still be pissed that we didn't invite you to the wedding."

"You didn't even tell us you were getting married," Carrick retorted.

Ronan listened to the oft repeated argument and tuned them out. He turned his head at the sound of his front door opening and noticed a shadow crossing his hallway. His boys were home and he hurried into the hall to see them standing statue still, looking up at the empty wall. Ronan uttered a quiet curse and skidded to a halt when he saw Joa standing in the open doorway, snow dusting her dark hair. The icy wind blew snow inside and Ronan shivered. He walked over to her, tugged her forward and pushed the door closed, looking from her to the boys. "Where's Tanna?"

Joa's big eyes flicked off the bare spot on the wall to his face and immediately went back again. "Um, she pulled up as I did. She was in a hurry to get back, so I brought the boys in."

Ronan nodded and went over to his boys, dropping to kiss each on his small head. "Hey, guys, did you have fun?"

Aron nodded enthusiastically and held up his arms to be picked up. Ronan hauled him up and settled him on his hip. "There was lots of ice cream and a horse and a clown—"

"Where's my mom gone?" Sam demanded.

Ronan tightened his grip on Aron as he dropped to his haunches to look Sam in the eye. "Your mom hasn't gone anywhere, Sam. I've just taken her painting off the wall, that's all."

"Why?"

Explanation time. *Hell.* "Because she's not here anymore and I think it's time we start to remember her in our hearts and minds and not because there's a huge picture on the wall."

"But what if I start to forget what she looks like?" Sam asked, panic in his voice.

"There's a photo of her next to your bed. You won't forget, Sam." Ronan darted a look at Joa. "We won't forget her, Sam, I promise."

Joa dropped her head to stare at the floor as Ronan pulled his older son in for a hug. "It's time, Sam."

Ronan felt Carrick remove Aron from his arms and he looked up to see Finn place his hand on Sam's shoulder. His younger brother waited for Sam to look up at him. "Hey, bud. Want to come home with me? We can have a movie and video game night."

They were supposed to be going out for supper with their new nanny but Ronan couldn't face it. Besides, he had something important to do, much to say.

Ronan stood up, pulled his phone from the back pocket of his jeans and quickly sent Abigail a text message, asking to postpone their arrangements for the evening. He saw that she'd read the message and then a thumbs-up emoji appeared on his screen.

Right, one very small mission accomplished.

Ronan returned his attention to the conversation between Sam and Finn, who were discussing what movie to watch.

"Popcorn?" Sam asked. His boys were such boys, Ronan thought. Easily distracted with the thought of junk food and some age-appropriate violence.

He sent Finn a grateful smile and looked at Aron. "Want to go and hang out with Finn, A?"

Aron shook his head and wound his arms around Carrick's neck. "Want to go with 'Rick."

Ronan arched his eyebrow at Carrick. His brother was in love and surely wanted to spend some alone time with Sadie. He expected Carrick to make an excuse. But Carrick just looked from Ronan to Joa and quickly nodded. "Sure, bud. We'll hang out."

It took a village—or, in his case, his brothers— to raise a child. God, he was lucky to have them. "Thanks, guys."

Ronan gave his boys another quick hug, sad to see them go after not seeing them for two days. But he and Joa had things to talk about, and they didn't need the distraction. They were only trying to sort out the rest of their lives…

After Carrick and Finn scooped up the boys and the bags they'd walked in with and left, each with a child in tow, Ronan took Joa's coat and hung it up on the coatrack.

Joa unwound her scarf, not sure what was happening. The boys had left, she didn't know if they were still going to dinner with Abigail and there was a damn big empty patch on the wall. Joa looked at the plastic-covered portrait and wondered whether she was hallucinating.

But no, there were two other boxes filled with— she lifted the open lid—more photographs. The wall going up the stairs was bare of photos and Thandi's scarf and hat weren't on the coatrack to the left of the door.

Joa looked at Ronan, so handsome, so serious.

"It was time."

Joa looked at him. "Really?"

Ronan nodded. Placing a hand on her arm, he tugged her over to the staircase and sat down on the third step up. He patted the spot next to him and Joa bit her lip, not sure what to do. She felt totally spacy, like she'd been tossed into an alternate reality where nothing made sense. She debated whether to sit or bolt. But Ronan's gaze was steady on her face and his beautiful, serious eyes begged her to trust him or, at the very least, to hear him out.

So she sat down, keeping a solid ten inches between them.

It took a few excruciating minutes for him to speak. "Thandi is a part of me, Ju. Death has marked me. I'd be lying if I told you it hasn't. Losing her ripped me apart, it really did."

"I know, Ronan. I mean, I don't *know* know but—" Joa's words tumbled out, desperate to reassure him. How lucky he was to know love like that, how lucky Thandi was to be loved so fully by this amazing man. How brave they'd both been.

Ronan's hand gripped hers and squeezed. "Just listen, please."

Joa expected him to remove his hand, but instead he just slid his fingers between hers, his palm warm against her skin.

"Thandi was amazing and I loved her very much and I want to remember her. She *deserves* to be remembered."

Joa tried to remain impassive, but Ronan must've seen the distress on her face because he squeezed her fingers gently. "I'm not trying to hurt you, sweetheart, but I need you to understand. Because if you don't, there's no hope for us. So will you try?"

God, didn't he know that she'd do anything for him? Not able to speak, Joa just nodded.

"It's taken me a long time to realize, to accept, that it's not all or nothing. We can't shove emotions into boxes and pull them out when we want. Death is far more complex than that and I need you to accept that I can still love and miss her and be totally, wildly, crazy in love with you."

Joa thought she heard that he loved her but that couldn't be right, could it? "I've been happier with you these last few weeks than I have been for years and I'd like to keep being that happy. But the thing is, I know I'll still think of her occasionally and I don't want you to feel threatened by that. I love her, but I'm not *in love* with her anymore.

"I'm so in love with you, though."

Joa stared, trying to make sense of what he'd said.

Could she love this man, knowing a part of him would always love his wife?

"Do you compare us?"

Ronan released a small snort. "Hell, no. You two are as different as night and day."

Well, that was a relief. Joa, needing to move, stood up and paced the area of the hallway in front of him, her thumbnail between her teeth. Could she do this, could she take a chance on him?

Ronan started to speak, but Joa shook her head, holding her hand in a silent plea to let her think.

She could walk away right now and resume her solitary life, hiding out behind her walls and not letting anyone get close. Or she could let Ronan in and give love a chance.

He was a good man, a sexy man and she loved him, she did. But could she play second fiddle? She needed to know…

"Do you think you can ever love me as much as you love her?" she whispered.

Ronan released a curse as he jumped to his feet, his expression revealing his distress. And at that moment, Joa understood. His expression told her that it wasn't a more or less kind of thing. It was equal but different and maybe she had the edge because she was, obviously, *here*.

Ronan cupped her face in his big hands. "Oh, Ju, not for one minute did I mean for you to think that it was a matter of levels. I just need you to understand that although I've put her away, although I've moved on because you stepped into my life, I am, occasionally, going to think about her. But I promise this won't be a three-person relationship. This is you and me."

"And the boys," Joa added, covering his hands with hers.

"Yeah, them," Ronan teased. "Do you understand? You will be my priority. I won't live in the past when I have you in my present."

"Ro…" Joa lifted her face, leaning on her toes for a kiss. Ronan's lips covered hers and Joa finally, finally felt like she was home, that she was part of something bigger and better than herself.

Then Ronan stepped back and his hands left her face to rest on her shoulders. His intense eyes bored into hers and Joa knew their conversation wasn't over, that it was her turn. Her man—so self-assured and confident—needed to know where he stood, whether he was as important to her as she was to him.

Joa held on to his wrists and briefly closed her eyes. Pulling in all her courage, she gave him the words he needed. No, the words she needed to say.

"I've been on my own for so long and I knew I wanted a family but I kept falling in love with un-available men. Because I was scared of the one thing I wanted most. Scared of being happy, of being loved, scared of losing that love. It's easier to be on your own, you know?"

Ronan squeezed her shoulders. "I do. Falling in love is terrifying."

"But I'd rather be scared with you than lonely on my own," Joa confessed. "I love you. I'd love you even if you didn't have those two monsters."

"Good to know," Ronan said, smiling. "Make you a deal?"

Joa tipped her head. "I'm listening."

"When you're feeling scared and overwhelmed, tell me and I'll remind you how much I love you. Look, Ju, I'm old enough to know that it's not going to be all roses and dancing on clouds. We both have a lot of baggage. But that's life. We're two strong people and I like us that way. But if we try to communicate, if we're brave enough to tell each other how we are feeling, *what* we are feeling, we can love each other through anything."

Joa felt the burn of tears, the warmth of happiness. She wound her arms around Ronan's neck and buried her nose in his neck. "I love you so much."

Ronan pulled her into him, one hand on her butt, another on her back. She felt safe and secure in his arms, like no one could touch her, like she'd never have to be alone again.

She had Ronan, Sam and Aron, and hopefully in a year or two, a child of her own. She jerked back, thinking she might as well start practicing her rusty communication skills as soon as possible. "I want a child," she said, her words rushing out. "Not today, or tomorrow, but sometime in the future."

Ronan didn't blink. He just pushed her hair behind her ears and nodded. "Sure."

Wow, okay. That was easy. While she was on a roll, she thought she'd raise another subject. "And I'm going to head up the foundation. I mean, I intend to help you raise Aron and Sam, but I want to work, Ro. It's important."

Ronan nodded. "I assumed so. That's why I hired Abigail. She starts on Monday."

Joa grinned at him. "So, no dinner tonight?"

Ronan's grin turned seductive and Joa felt the special place between her legs heat up. "Oh, there will be dinner. And you're on the menu."

"Really? That sounds interesting."

Ronan's lips curved as his mouth descended toward hers. "Mmm, I need to practice making babies."

Joa laughed, happiness a new, foreign and completely wonderful feeling "Yeah, I think you've proved you can do that, Murphy."

"Boy babies, maybe. Girl babies take a little more practice."

Ronan led her up the stairs and then up another flight of stairs. He paused outside his bedroom door, his eyes green and gold and blue. He cupped the back of her neck with his big hand and rested his forehead against hers. "I want you in my bed, Ju. Just you and me, a blank page, the start of a new chapter. Will you come inside with me?"

Of course she would. She would go anywhere with him. Because, as she knew, as he'd just proved, fairy tales could come true.

Epilogue

Murphy International often held a presale cocktail party the evening before an important auction and the world's foremost collectors of Fabergé were present, peering through glass cases to look at the items going on the block the next day.

Joa, like everybody else, had done her fair share of drooling over the objects she'd first laid eyes on in the vault somewhere way below her feet in the bowels of the building. But she kept coming back to the miniature egg, dotted with diamonds and rubies, edged with gold. She'd asked Keely if she could pull Isabel's miniature egg pendant from the Mounton sale and Keely had agreed. Joa touched the silver egg that hung in the deep, plunging V of her black cocktail dress and wondered if she could justify owning two miniature eggs by Fabergé.

She was rich, but she wasn't—she hoped—spoiled.

But damn, it was beautiful.

Joa felt Ronan's possessive touch on her back and smiled when he dropped a hot kiss on her bare shoulder. Tipping her head to rest it against his, she sent up a quick prayer of intense gratitude…

For this man, for his boys, for her completely extraordinary life.

"Careful, darling, you're drooling," Ronan said, wrapping his arm around her waist.

Joa leaned into him. "I know, but it's utterly fantastic." She bit her lip and shrugged. "I'm thinking of buying it at the auction tomorrow."

Ronan lifted one eyebrow. "It's your money, darling. You can do anything you damn well like." Then he winced, as if remembering something. "But maybe I should tell you that I've just heard that this pendant has been withdrawn from the sale by the owner."

Joa's shoulders slumped in disappointment. "Aw, no. Seriously?"

Joa saw Finn and Keely approaching them but, as per normal, quickly returned her attention to Ronan, looking utterly debonair in his classic black tuxedo. The shadows from his eyes were gone and his sensuous mouth was quick to smile. She'd done that, she thought, proud.

She'd made him happy and she intended to keep doing that—she glanced down at her simple engagement ring with its huge diamond—for the rest of her life. Not being able to buy this pendant was the first blip on her completely perfect life.

Maybe she *was* becoming spoiled...

"Has it been sold to someone else?" Joa demanded. "Can I make a counteroffer?"

Ronan shook his head. "Sorry. The new buyer has no intention of selling it. It's a gift to someone he loves with all his heart and soul."

"What are you two discussing so intently?" Keely demanded, stopping next to Joa. Then she wrinkled her nose. "But if it's anything mushy, you can skip the explanation."

"Yeah," Finn agreed, "between you two and Carrick and Sadie, and Tanna and Levi, you're making the rest of us feel nauseous."

"I agree! What's with the constant PDA? Can't you keep your hands off each other for more than a millisecond?" Keely demanded.

"Shut up," Ronan genially told them, not taking his eyes off Joa, whose heart was bouncing around her rib cage. Ronan was teasing her about something, she was sure of it...

What was he up to?

Finn bent down to look at the pendant before standing up and looking at Ronan. "Is this the pendant you bought off the Fabergé collector?"

Ronan released a loud groan. "Jesus, Finn! It was supposed to be a surprise!"

Finn pulled a face at Joa. "Oh. Sorry."

"Go away," Ronan told him through gritted teeth. Joa watched his brother and her best friend walk away, idly noticing that they both darted glances across the room. Finn was looking for Beah and Keely was glaring at Dare...

Situation normal, Joa thought.

Bringing her attention back to her fiancé, she lifted her eyebrows. "Did you really buy this pendant for someone you love with all your heart and soul?"

Ronan cupped the side of her face with his big hand and Joa turned to kiss the palm of his hand. "Yeah, I plan on giving her one as often as I can..."

"That could be quite expensive," Joa murmured as Ronan's mouth moved toward hers.

"Trust me, she's worth every damn cent. She's, quite simply, my life."

As he was hers.

"Thank you, Ro."

And they both knew she wasn't just thanking him for the pendant but also for giving her a place to belong, for giving her a forever family.

* * * * *

Finn Murphy's older brothers have found their soul mates. He's happy for them, but won't follow in their footsteps. He was married once. It was a disaster.

But when his ex-wife, Beah Jenkinson, falls back into Finn's life, their attraction burns hotter than before...

Will Finn make the same mistake twice?

Find out in

Back in His Ex's Bed

Available June 2020!

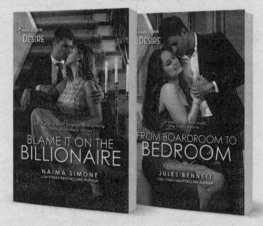

#2731 CLAIMED BY A STEELE

Forged of Steele • by Brenda Jackson

When it comes to settling down, playboy CEO Gannon Steele has a ten-year plan. And it doesn't include journalist Delphine Ryland. So why is he inviting her on a cross-country trip? Especially since their red-hot attraction threatens to do away with all his good intentions...

#2732 HER TEXAS RENEGADE

Texas Cattleman's Club: Inheritance • by Joanne Rock

When wealthy widow and business owner Miranda Dupree needs a security expert, there's only one person for the job—her ex, bad boy hacker Kai Maddox. It's all business until passions reignite, but will her old flame burn her a second time?

#2733 RUTHLESS PRIDE

Dynasties: Seven Sins • by Naima Simone

Putting family first, CEO Joshua Lowell abandoned his dreams to save his father's empire. When journalist Sophie Armstrong uncovers a shocking secret, he'll do everything in his power to shield his family from another scandal. But wanting her is a complication he didn't foresee...

#2734 SCANDALOUS REUNION

Lockwood Lightning • by Jules Bennett

Financially blackmailed attorney Maty Taylor must persuade her ex, Sam Hawkins, to sell his beloved distillery to his enemy. His refusal does nothing to quiet the passion between Maty and Sam. When powerful secrets are revealed, can their second chance survive?

#2735 AFTER HOURS SEDUCTION

The Men of Stone River • by Janice Maynard

When billionaire CEO Quinten Stone is injured, he reluctantly accepts live-in help at his remote home from assistant Katie Duncan—who he had a passionate affair with years earlier. Soon he's fighting his desire for the off-limits beauty as secrets from their past resurface...

#2736 SECRETS OF A FAKE FIANCÉE

The Stewart Heirs • by Yahrah St. John

Rejected by the family she wants to know, Morgan Stewart accepts Jared Robinson's proposal to pose as his fiancée to appease his own family. But when their fake engagement uncovers real passion, can Morgan have what she's always wanted, or will a vicious rumor derail everything?

HDCNM0420

SPECIAL EXCERPT FROM

⬡ HARLEQUIN
DESIRE

Putting family first, CEO Joshua Lowell abandoned his dreams to save his father's empire. When journalist Sophie Armstrong uncovers a shocking secret, he'll do everything in his power to shield his family and his pride from another scandal. But wanting her is a complication he didn't foresee…

Read on for a sneak peek at
Ruthless Pride
by USA TODAY bestselling author Naima Simone

"Stalking me, Ms. Armstrong?" he drawled, his fingers gripping his water bottle so tight, the plastic squeaked in protest.

He immediately loosened his hold. Damn, he'd learned long ago to never betray any weakness of emotion. People were like sharks scenting bloody chum in the water when they sensed a chink in his armor. But when in this woman's presence, his emotions seemed to leak through like a sieve. The impenetrable shield barricading him that had been forged in the fires of pain, loss and humiliation came away dented and scratched after an encounter with Sophie. And that presented as much of a threat, a danger to him, as her insatiable need to prove that he was a deadbeat father and puppet to a master thief.

"Stalking you?" she scoffed, bending down to swipe her own bottle of water and a towel off the ground. "Need I remind you, it was you who showed up at my job yesterday, not the other way around. So I guess that makes us even in the showing-up-where-we're-not-wanted department."

"Oh, we're not even close to anything that resembles even, Sophie," he said, using her name for the first time aloud. And damn if it didn't taste good on his tongue. If he didn't sound as if he were stroking the two syllables like they were bare, damp flesh.

"I hate to disappoint you and your dreams of narcissistic grandeur, but I've been a member of this gym for years." She swiped her towel over her throat and upper chest. "I've seen you here, but it's not my fault if you've never noticed me."

"That's bull," he snapped. "I would've noticed you."

The words echoed between them, the meaning in them pulsing like a thick, heavy heartbeat in the sudden silence that cocooned them. Her silver eyes flared wide before they flashed with…what? Surprise? Irritation? Desire. A liquid slide of lust prowled through him like a hungry—so goddamn hungry—beast.

The air simmered around them. How could no one else see it shimmer in waves from the concrete floor like steam from a sidewalk after a summer storm?

She was the first to break the visual connection, and when she ducked her head to pat her arms down, the loss of her eyes reverberated in his chest like a physical snapping of tautly strung wire. He fisted his fingers at his side, refusing to rub the echo of soreness there.

"Do you want me to pull out my membership card to prove that I'm not some kind of stalker?" She tilted her head to the side. "I'm dedicated to my job, but I refuse to cross the line into creepy…or criminal."

He ground his teeth against the apology that shoved at his throat, but after a moment, he jerked his head down in an abrupt nod. "I'm sorry. I shouldn't have jumped to conclusions." And then because he couldn't resist, because it still gnawed at him when he shouldn't have cared what she—a reporter—thought of him or not, he added, "That predilection seems to be in the air."

She narrowed her eyes on him, and a tiny muscle ticked along her delicate but stubborn jaw. Why that sign of temper and forced control fascinated him, he opted not to dwell on. "And what is that supposed to mean?" she asked, the pleasant tone belied by the anger brewing in her eyes like gray storm clouds.

Moments earlier, he'd wondered if fury or desire had heated her gaze.

God help him, because masochistic fool that he'd suddenly become, he craved them both.

He wanted her rage, her passion…wanted both to beat at him, heat his skin, touch him. Make him feel.

Mentally, he scrambled away from that, that need, like it'd reared up and flashed its fangs at him. The other man he'd been—the man who'd lost himself in passion paint and life captured on film—had drowned in emotion. Willingly. Joyfully. And when it'd been snatched away—when that passion, that life—had been stolen from him by cold, brutal reality, he'd nearly crumbled under the loss, the darkness. Hunger, wanting something so desperately, led only to the pain of eventually losing it.

He'd survived that loss once. Even though it'd been like sawing off his own limbs. He might be an emotional amputee, but dammit, he'd endured. He'd saved his family, their reputation and their business. But he'd managed it by never allowing himself to need again.

And Sophie Armstrong, with her pixie face and warrior spirit, wouldn't undo all that he'd fought and silently screamed to build.

Don't miss what happens next in…
Ruthless Pride by Naima Simone,
the first in the Dynasties: Seven Sins series,
where passion may be the only path to redemption.

Available May 2020 wherever
Harlequin Desire books and ebooks are sold.

Harlequin.com